CHAPTER II

We had an extremely good supper, and our snug little party of four thoroughly enjoyed it. Everything that could tempt and pamper the appetite was there—game of several varieties, and oysters and other shellfish served in the most exquisite style. I couldn't help thinking that if the ladies in the convent lived on such luxurious and exciting viands, it was no wonder that they found their blood a little hotter and their passions more excitable than was consistent with their religious vows. And indeed the effects of the highly dressed dishes, and fine wines of which Father Eustace partook liberally, as did my mother and aunt, began to make themselves visible. I was inclined to resent the very affectionate manner displayed by the handsome confessor towards my mother; but the Abbess, perceiving what was passing in my mind, motioned me into an adjoining room, and there made me understand that the reverend was most probably my own father. Indeed she was quite sure of it.

"In fact," she said, "I would stake my reputation,

my dear Auguste, that Monsieur d'Ermonville is not."

"How do you know that, my dear aunt," I asked.

"Oh, by the simplest way in the world," she laughingly replied. "Very soon after my sister was married, I went to call upon her. She was out, but I was informed that monsieur would be happy to receive me, and so indeed he appeared to be. He paid me the highest compliments about my face and general appearance, and I suppose he was right, for I was then a novice in the convent and appeared very provocative in my simple. Of course, it was sixteen years ago. I was much younger and handsomer than I am now."

"You are lovely now, my darling aunt!" I exclaimed, thrusting myself upon her, kissing her lasciviously and running my hands over her ripe body.

"Spare me your lust for the present, my dear Auguste," said she, "and let me finish my story. After supper you shall amuse yourself as much as you like."

Seating herself on my knee, and permitting my hand to retain the position where it had settled between her thighs, she continued:

"Your reputed father proceeded from compliments to kissing, and from kissing to feeling and handling my breasts and rump, which for a girl of sixteen were really very well developed. Of course I could have prevented all of it if I had wanted, but I was very far from being the innocent girl I looked. My handsome young confessor had long since taken care of all that. Still, I thought it right to make some faint protest, but was met by the assertion that it was all in the family and was right and proper. He then lifted my clothes up, and had a close inspection of all I had to show. Indeed he had more, for he spread my delicate cunt lips with his fingers and began to lick me. The sensation was maddening. He kept my slit spread apart until he found the delicate nob of flesh that soon stood to his attention at the insistence of his tongue. My clit—indeed my entire body—quivered with each

24

slash upon it. He nibbled and bit it, alternating these attentions with plunging deeply into my gaping cunt-hole. When he was finished with this, I pretended to sink down on the sofa as if quite helpless, with my thighs falling apart.

Now was the worthy old nobleman's time. He man-fully took down his breeches and out came his thick tool. Unfortunately, I saw out of the corner of my half shut eyes that it was of no use, not a bit of it! His cock might have been a good one at some time or another, and it was not so bad in appearance even now, only it would not stand! That was a fatal defect. He lay upon me, passed his hand under my bottom, and felt me there. Then raised himself and contemplated my wide-open charms. But it made no difference; his prick would not stiffen. So at last I got up from the sofa in a state of great disgust and disappointment, and sincere pity for your poor mother, who, as I sub-sequently discovered, found spiritual and bodily con-solation in the ministrations of Father Eustace. So you must never mind his being lovingly attentive to your mother, my dear Auguste. And now," said she, kissing me, "if you have quite done rummaging my secret parts, we will return to the supper room."

Very much relieved by this disclosure, I returned to the parlor in high spirits, and found my mother and her confessor laughing merrily at something they had been discussing. Immediately upon our entrance, Father Eustace said to me, "I have been telling your mother in your absence, mademoiselle, that it is my duty as one of the principal confessors appointed to the Convent of Saint Claire to make proper enquiry as to the morals and habits of all its inmates even when not professed nuns or even novices. I think the presence of your mother and aunt will rid the pro-ceedings of all impropriety. Undoubtedly, the Abbess has completely satisfied her mind as to your sex and purity, but I should like to satisfy myself, just for form's sake you know. So Mademoiselle Augustine, I will trouble you to come near to me and take up your petticoats."

At this I hesitated considerably, but my mother from the other side of the table nodded and smiled at me, and my aunt whispered, "Go to him. It is only fun!" So I went around to the side of the table where his reverence was sitting with his arm around my mother's waist, and deliberately lifted my petticoats. This displayed to the delight—but not to the surprise—of all present, my fine cock and its dangling balls in all their glory. Indeed my prick had been more or less stiff ever since I had entered the convent walls. There had been a temporary lull during supper, but feeling my aunt's cunt and hearing her lascivious story had brought the hardness on again with increased vigor, and I felt as if I should burst. I reddened as my mother laughed, and Agatha came from her side of the table to have a nearer view, but Father Eustace preserved his solemn manner and laid hold of my throbbing cock as if was ascertaining the weight and measurement of it. Finally, on trying to force it downwards from its upright standard, and failing, he turned around to my mother, saying with approval, "He is his father's own son."

"Certainly, dear Eustace," replied my mother. "I am glad that you recall your youth in him again."

"Well," replied the priest, "I am not so old that I can't raise my prick up. In spite of all the nuns and novices I have fucked in the course of my duty, I am far from being worn out yet. Look here, young gentleman!" he ordered. "You are not full grown yet, and, I doubt not, will become much larger. But I hardly think you will ever be able to show such a lordly tool as mine."

So saying he rose up, and opening his robe disclosed an enormous dark-hued, purple-topped weapon, that, but for the color, would not have disgraced a donkey. His balls were more like those of a young bull than anything human. But the ladies weren't afraid. On the contrary, they regarded us with looks of admiration and longing. My aunt even passed her arm around my neck and whispered, "Your father's is larger, dear Auguste, and Henriette is welcome to it. I prefer yours."

Father Eustace ended the exhibition by saying, "I take great interest in you, young gentleman; you are the son of a beautiful lady who is very dear to me." At this my mother gave him a loving and grateful glance. "Under other circumstances such a bold experiment as you have ventured upon might have cost you your life. Yet, I will grant you such privileges as are never accorded except to the legitimate shepherds of the flock, such as priests, monks, confessors, and such like, always in the performance of their duty."

Here I fancied he winked at the Mother Superior, and she certainly laughed. However, he went on to say that I might have the run of the convent as far as the young ladies were concerned, both nuns and novices. He was not much afraid of scandal, for evil days were coming and the Convent of Ste. Claire would be suppressed among others, so that he didn't much care if all the pretty young nuns and novices had their virginity taken.

"By the way, Sister Agatha," he continued, "are there any maids in the Convent now...pretty ones I mean?"

"Oh yes," replied my aunt, "a few. There's Louise and Agnes of course—she is very strict indeed. And I believe the novice Adele has never had a man between her thighs, though I have reason to think she has lost her maidenhead."

"I suppose she has to thank your ladyship for that," said Father Eustace, smiling.

"Certainly," replied my aunt in a businesslike way,

"I wanted to amuse myself, and thought it would do her good."

"Oh, of course," said he, "you are privileged to do as you like. Well, about this fine lad, let him do as he likes among them, only let him wear this pretty dress still—it will cause less scandal and gain him entry to all the recesses of the convent. Then you may turn him loose among them like a young stag among a herd of does."

"Not before he spends a night with me," hastily interposed my aunt.

"Oh, Agatha, you ought to be ashamed of yourself," exclaimed my mother, while Father Eustace laughed loudly and remarked that fucking between relatives so near of kin was not allowed by the Canons of the church!

While this was going on, my aunt whispered to me, "I will grant you every pleasure that you can possibly conceive!" To which I breathed in reply, "Indeed my beautiful aunt, I long to throw you down the sofa and split you up this very minute!"

By this time Father Eustace, who had imbibed a good deal of wine, recovered from his fit of laughter and said, "But damn the Canons of the Church! I never cared about them, and if they do away with them and the Church too, I don't much care. I'll get a commission in the army! And so, my dear lad, you may fuck your Aunt Agatha if you have a fancy for it. She is really a very splendid woman and I'll give you a dispensation for poking an Abbess. Mind you do it with vigor and style though, or she will never forgive you. Indeed, you had better give her a few inches in the presence of your beautiful mother and myself. We are both good judges and I should like to see if you resemble me in other particulars besides the mere length of your prick."

To this my mother objected, saying it was really too indelicate, but nobody minded her. Indeed Father

Eustace began to smother her with such a volley of voluptuous kisses that I could plainly see that Agatha's was not the only pussy that was going to be plumbed. He wasted no time going about setting an example—for he had no trouble (as I often did) of taking up a silk robe and a lot of petticoats, or of fastening them up. He had already opened his robe in front, laid my mother on a couch, and taking her legs upon his arms, proceeded to administer his terrible weapon in a most forcible manner. He thrust his hips forward until the head of his enormous cock butted at her thickly-forested entrance. Without the used of his hand he forced the swollen bulb past the taut lips which slid easily apart to receive it. Once it was secured within he withheld himself for a moment as if savoring the sensation. He wriggled his rump about and rotated his hips so that the pink helmet buried in the slit opened the passage. Then, with one driving thrust, he plunged the entire length of the shaft into her up to his very balls. These slapped her upturned buttocks as he commenced a savage fucking, ramming the pole into her again and again until I thought my mother would scream.

Anxious as Agatha and I both were to commence fucking on our own account, we could not help watching the amorous conflict taking place on the other sofa. At last, impatient to begin, I said, "If you will kneel down, my lovely aunt, in what is called dog fashion, I shall be able to fuck you in most gallant style and admire all the delights you have to display. At the same time both of us will be able to admire from our posture the delightful spectacle on the other couch."

She did so and I quickly moved behind her smoothly rounded buttocks. I separated these half-moons with my hands, bringing my throbbing cock to the head of the slit that peered shyly at me from underneath. Anxious to emulate Father Eustace, I forced my way within with little preamble. Nor did I hesitate once the aching head of my cock was trapped inside that tight pussy. Instead I immediately thrust within, feeling every inch of my rod working its tenacious way deeper and deeper into my aunt's love passage.

"Give it to her Auguste! Give it to her, my son!" said Father Eustace, as he watched my frenzied ministration.

As he said this he drew out about six inches of his massive cock from my mother's cunt, then plunged it in again to the hilt, eliciting from her an exclamation and a plea to be more gentle. But there was not much gentleness from either father or son; nor from the ladies when our ramming motions began to produce their proper results. After a minute or two, Mother began to toss her legs in the air in the style of an acrobat, while my aunt lifted up her rump to meet my heavy thrusts as if she wanted my cock to be twice as long as it was. Oh, I fucked her long and hard. I continued to withdraw and thrust, withdraw and thrust, until I feared my cock should emerge from my aunt's mouth from the force of my rammings. It was exquisite, and I soon felt the mounting pressure in my balls and shaft that indicated an imminent eruption. In a moment I was spurting jets of thick creme into the eager receptacle while my body spasmed from the peaking activity.

Well, all pleasures come to an end, and the ecstatic delights of entering the body of a lovely woman are among the briefest of all. All of us lay on separate couches tolerably exhausted. The ladies lay in most lascivious attitudes with spread legs that openly displayed their oozing pussies.

Certainly, I thought, reflecting dreamily, this is rather a strange predicament for a young man—To find himself in feminine dress, fucking the Lady Superior of a strict Convent, and which Lady being his own aunt! At the same time witnessing his mother being outrageously fucked in the same room by her confessor, whom I found to be my own bodily father! It is rather a strange adventure.

Father Eustace was the first to recover himself. Like the expert practitioner he was he recommended that we two give the partners a bumper of champagne to restore their animation.

"And let's not forget ourselves, my son," said he. "Here's your health! Remember that I'll keep an eye upon you and assist you if ever I have a chance, or if you have need of it."

I thanked him and pledged his health, after helping my lovely aunt to rearrange her garments. The last piece of advice Father Eustace gave me on parting for the night was to take a few more stewed oysters. He added, with a sly glance at my aunt, "Her ladyship has only made a beginning. You'll have quite a bit to go through before morning, I suspect. I hope you'll find it pleasant! Good night!"

CHAPTER III

I took Father Eustace's good advice, and shortly afterwards our little party broke up. My mother and his Reverence found suitable accommodations for themselves, and my handsome hostess took me with her into her own bedroom.

There I found two baths—slightly perfumed—awaiting us. We both stripped and bathed. From this luxurious operation I experienced most beneficial effects, and so did my aunt. Indeed, as we were wiping ourselves and each other we both became as lively as if the lovemaking we had just performed on the sofa had been a matter of no consequence at all.

My Lady Abbess was soon to perceive the effect produced upon me. She asked me to dry her back with a soft towel. Of course I was happy to be of service. I continued the operation from her back downwards to her magnificent buttocks which I gently separated and moulded like firm dough, paying due attention to the small orifice there located. From there my hands roamed to the moss-covered receptacle which my cock had recently occupied. Of course the least I could do was to pay particular attention to this spot, and in the course of handling it and drying it my prick began to stand as savagely as if I had not seen a pretty woman for six months.

As I was stark naked, Madame Agatha was not slow to perceive this interesting fact, and exclaimed, "Oh, you darling boy, how ready and manful you are! I was afraid that I should have to take the rod to you, or resort to some other of the means by which women restore vitality to the dormant powers of our male friends. But you don't require anything of the kind." At this point she actually knelt down and began handling and kissing my shaft and balls until I began to fear that my sperm would be wasted on her face, when it ought to be injected elsewhere. When I hinted at this, she reluctantly withdrew, saying that she didn't want to lose a precious drop on any account and begged me to follow her to bed instantly.

I wanted to ask her a good many questions, one in particular about the rod she spoke of, but I saw that talking was perfectly useless until I had satisfied her animal lusts. Although my performance upon her upturned bottom had been very delightful, and had worked her up to a high pitch of excitement, yet it had made her desire for me even greater. To speak more plainly, although I had the satisfaction of injecting a most copious amount of my fluid into her eager pussy, she herself had not come. So my aunt had got just enough to make her want more.

She even avoided all gentle preliminaries such as I believe women generally like. No sooner were we in bed she drew me to her. I was determined, however, not to give her the immediate and fleeting satisfaction she craved by plunging my rock-hard piston into her hungry cunt. Instead I moved up and guided my jerking shaft to the lips of her mouth, forcing it past her teeth and into her throat. Without objection she took it all and slurped all around the shaft, head and balls while I commenced a steady, rocking motion. I remained buried in her throat for quite some while, feeling my cock swelling until I was sure she would be unable to breathe. Then I withdrew it and gave her what she so desperately desired, driving it between the lips of her slit and burying it up to my balls.

Two or three more stalwart shoves on my part, followed by some ecstatic heavings and boundings on Agatha's part, a few rapturous exclamations from both of us, and I felt my cock saturated up to the very roots with warm foaming cream. Two seconds laster I spurted my load into her grasping cunt. Her tight lips wrung every last drop from me as I spasmed in a paroxysm of ecstasy. We both lay for a minute or two, my aunt kissed me, and called me all the endearing names she could think of in gratitude for my successful performance. Being rather practical as far as my own comforts are concerned, I put a stop to this proceeding by suggesting the propriety of covering ourselves somewhat, which was immediately followed by her producing two elegant nightdresses, which we put on before returning to bed. Not being very sleepy however, I asked my lovely bed-fellow to tell me what she meant by her allusion to the "rod" and why she talked of applying it to me.

"To you, dearest Auguste, I can perceive it will be quite an unnecessary instrument," she replied. "But we occasionally have to use it both on the buttocks of our male friends, and the soft white rumps of our young ladies. It is merely a birch rod," said she, opening a drawer near her bed and producing one. "And these," she continued, throwing on the bed a lot of velvet-covered straps and buckles, "are what we sometimes use to confine a novice's arms and legs, if she proves reluctant. Surely you must know, you innocent boy, that the application of the rod excites the lust of both the whipper and the whipped...the latter to a most wonderful extent.

In the Convent of St. Emergarde, where I first entered the service of the Lord, our favorite confessor, Father Abelard, was often requested by our Lady Superior to favor her with his company at supper, as soon as his duties were concluded. By this time you're aware, dear Auguste, that the 'duties' of a confessor do not always consist of hearing a pretty girl repeat a litany of nonsense about the sins she has been guilty of for a week or two past."

"No, indeed," said I. "The glorious scene between Father Eustace and Emilie would satisfy me to the contrary."

"Well," said my fair instructress, "I have known Father Abelard to fuck three of the finest novices on one afternoon, and then with our Mother Superior. By now you also know, Auguste, that the Superior is not necessarily either the ugliest, oldest, or most devout woman in the convent, and our Lady Beatrice was a handsome and a very lascivious woman. On the present occasion Father Abelard had not been in her private apartment ten minutes before her bell rang furiously, and I was requested to bring the rod forthwith. I may here mention that I had experienced the effect of that weapon, and was regarded, although quite a novice, as one of the initiated. How this happened I will tell you shortly, although not until I finish my story.

"First I asked the Abbess if she required my personal attentions, but she replied, 'Most certainly not,' and by way of showing that she was perfectly ready, placed herself on the edge of the bed, half reclining, half sitting, with each leg supported by a chair and as wide apart as they could stretch. Between those beautiful ivory shafts we placed Father Abelard, leaning over her and kissing her, and sticking out his rump so as to have the full benefit of my ministrations.

"I, who recollected my initiation in the ways of the rod from Father Abelard two months before did not spare him! I let him have it handsomely upon the buttocks with the rod. After a few smart strokes, my superior called out, 'That's right, give it to him well. His cock is beginning to stand finely!' I repeated my endeavors until slight blood streaks began to show upon the healthy taut skin of his muscular posterior. At last having attained the stiffness required, he took his prick in hand and shoved it well into the lady's burning cunt whose lips had long been gaping open. He thrust like a madman, varying his motion little except to raise himself up from time to time so as to increase the force of his next downward thrust. I continued to stroke his buttocks with the switch, which only served to heighten the effect of his pleasure as he scoured her innermost sanctum with his ravaging prick. At last he seemed to lose all control and I knew he was injecting that warm envelope with the flood of his passion.

After the termination of their encounter, the Mother Superior expressed herself as greatly obliged to me, and granted me indulgence to remain in bed until breakfast time next morning. This privilege was much valued by us novices, and I thanked her and retired, leaving them to their repose; which I don't doubt Father Abelard very much needed."

I was exceedingly amused by this story, particularly as I was totally ignorant of such things as birchings and whippings. But my curiosity was aroused, and I begged my instructress to give me an account of the violence to which she had been subjected during her novitiate. To this she at first objected; saying that she hoped I would embrace her a little more before morning came to separate us and that if I went to sleep I might awake refreshed and strong. But I suggested that her giving me an account of what happened to her on the occasion referred to would certainly excite my lustful feelings to an immense extent and she would benefit greatly from it.

With this charming prospect in view she consented and proceeded with her story.

"I was just sixteen when I commenced my novitiate. I was remarkably tall and well made for my age. Indeed I have seen many girls of eighteen who could not show such breasts, bottoms, or legs as I could at sixteen. And I have no doubt too that I was prematurely gifted with womanly passions, for I was frequently troubled with pleasant, yet unsatisfied dreams. In fact, I would often wake to find my private parts and my chemise wet, and yet myself not even half gratified. When alone, I used to meditate upon the various young monks who used to visit the convent, wondering which of them I liked best, and why.

"Now our Lady Beatrice noticed all this, for she was a woman not only experienced in herself, but very quick to notice any peculiarities in the young ladies under her charge. I suppose some sort of an arrangement to alleviate these needs is often entered into between an abbess and her favorite confessors. As for me, since I have held that responsible position I can safely say that I have never yet 'sold' one of the young ladies under my care. At the most, I may have given a hint to a favorite male friend that such a novice or nun exhibited signs of great heat, and that I should have to administer a dildo. Of course, if the priest thought that he could gain the girl's affections and try the effect of his own fleshy dildo, good and well. But I never yet resorted to the violence to which I was subjected when a girl.

"It happened this way: I was working at some embroidery one morning in the novices' parlour, when a message came to say that I was wanted in the Mother Superior's private apartments. To hear was to obey, and I presented myself immediately with a low

37

curtsey, not only to the Abbess but to two young monks who were in her apartments. One I knew well as Father Abelard, Lady Beatrice's favorite confessor, the other, a much younger man, I knew only slightly by sight. I know him much better now, he was no other than Eustace, who is at this moment either revelling or sleeping in my sister's arms in the adjoining room. By the Mother Superior I was received graciously, but my appearance seemed to revive some dispute between the two monks.

"'It is my right and I will maintain it,' said Abelard.

"'You will have many opportunities,' retorted Eustace, 'and her ladyship here promised me the first. Besides I have given an offering to the shrine of St. Emengarde.'

"'Much you care about the shrine,' said the other jeeringly, 'The shrine you care about is that situated between a pretty novice's plump thighs!'

"'Reverend Fathers both,' interposed the Abbess, 'I beg to remind you that this altercation is most unseemly and will produce a bad impression on the mind of my fair young novice here.' With this she nodded to them, looking towards me with a strongly marked impression as if recommending prudence.

"'Cannot you draw lots?' said she, 'I have a better idea still.' She said something to them in a low tone which seemed to amuse them and ended their dispute.

"'I agree,' said Abelard.

"'And I also,' said Eustace. 'Indeed, I may rather prefer the rear just by way of a change.'

"'Very well,' said the Abbess, 'So that you are agreed. I suppose she had better be stripped?'

"'Oh, certainly, stark naked, all but her stockings and slippers,' they both exclaimed, 'and she had better be slightly whipped just to tickle and excite her, not to hurt her much. And as you are sure she is a virgin, holy sister, you had better supply us with some cold cream or ointment to ease our passage, or we shall be shooting our sperm before we are half in her orifices.' And they both laughed as if there was some excellent joke. Now half of this was Greek to me, but I dimly understood that there was something about stripping and whipping, to be followed probably by other proceedings, in which it seemed both the reverend gentlemen proposed to participate.

"So although I was far from being a prude, it was with some reluctance that I obeyed my Mother Superior's orders to strip myself naked for inspection. But I had little choice in the matter, so I proceeded to unveil my charms. In a minute or two I stood exposed to the admiring but lustful gaze of the two spiritual directors.

"They immediately commenced their investigations. 'A very fine girl indeed.' 'Only sixteen you say, Lady Beatrice?' 'Hm! Looks rather older.' 'And a virgin, eh? Let us see.' These disjointed sentences fell from the lips of both the monks as they felt me and pulled me about, apparently in great delight.

"At last by way of inspecting my virginity, they both knelt down, one in front, and the other behind me. Abelard opened the taut lips of my cunt, and inspecting it and inserting his finger, remarked, 'I believe you are right, Sister Beatrice, and that she is still in possession of her maidenhead.'

"'She exhibits no signs of straining here,' responded Eustace from the other side, pulling open the cheeks of my rump, and inserting his finger into that puckered orifice, 'and what's more, I shall certainly require lots of cold cream or something of that sort, if I am to effect an entrance into that delicate little spot.'

"I felt a little frightened at these proceedings, despite my curiosity; and another feeling began to take some hold upon my imagination, as the gentlemen moved around me and knelt down. For I could get glimpses of what I had never seen before, namely a man's cock fully erect. The sight of those glorious, ruby-headed pricks certainly excited a little fear, but more admiration. In short, I was rapidly becoming exited, and would have consented willingly to anything in moderation. But, of course, moderation was unknown to my intending violators, and as for my own consent, they neither asked for it or required it.

They asked the Abbess if she thought it would be necessary to tie me down, to which she answered: 'Oh no! I don't think she will make any resistance, will you, Agatha? It is only an ordeal that all novices have to go through—all the desirable ones at any rate. It won't hurt you very much, if at all.'

"'Certainly not," chimed in the lustful monks. "We whip the pretty girls very lightly and fuck them very hard. The ugly ones we whip very hard and fuck very little; only just enough to keep them in health.'

"And they both chuckled over the ludicrous idea. As they were speaking, the Abbess had me kneel down on a divan somewhat similar to that on which you saw Emilie undergo her punishment. My placing myself in this position called forth from the monks renewed compliments on my beauty in general and the voluptuous swell of my buttocks in particular. But it was quite evident that the holy fathers could not contain themselves much longer. Abelard, seizing the birch rod, began to apply it, so gently at first that it did little more than tickle me, so that I rather liked it. But he got so excited by lust and by my exclamations, that he began to lay the weapon on much harder until I began to cry out. He switched me thoroughly, over my belly and back. Indeed, that was the very worst part of it, for the hissing undercuts he made caught the edges of my pussy lips and seemed to lay them raw. This only seemed to excite the monk to a greater degree, and he laid to with gusto, delighted in the way the scarlet streaks criss-crossed my tender flesh and reached to the borders of my private parts. At last, Lady Beatrice interposed, saying that I was a very good girl, and did not require such treatment and that she was sure I was quite ready to receive all they were able to give me.

"'Indeed you must stop the rod, brother Abelard,' interposed Father Eustace, who right before my eyes had been rubbing the scarlet knob of his cock until it shone. 'I won't have that lovely rump sacrificed any more. Recollect that I am going in there. A little tickling and smarting and a few red stripes I don't mind, but I shan't have the little darling's lovely posteriors made bloody. So grease your cock a little, and let us get our beauty between us. It's been a long time since we shared a fine girl.'

"'Not since you two nearly knocked my two holes into one, greedy wretches that you were!' laughed the Abbess. 'Agatha, stand here," she continued, 'with your back towards the edge of the bed. Now, Eustace, you stand half supported by the bed. You had better grease her bottomhole as well as your own huge piston! You, Abelard, get in front of her. Agatha, open your thighs! The wider you stretch them the less pain you will feel. You will very likely be lifted off your legs, but these lascivious gentlemen will manage to hold you up between them, I dare say.'

"Imagine my position!" said my aunt. "Whipped, naked, with both orifices greased and gaping to receive a pair of throbbing cocks, reclining slightly backwards on Father Eustace who was resting against the bed, with the tip of his cock already knocking for admittance at my back entrance. Meanwhile Abelard was in front, pulling open the lips of my lightly-downed cunt.

At last the time had come, and both began to push in together, but not far. Eustace found his channel of operations unexpectedly tight, and Father Abelard

41

was having difficulty proceeding past the barrier of my maidenhead.

"At this picture, the Abbess, who seemed half beside herself with lascivious delight, was of great service to them. She told Eustace that he need not be afraid of hurting me, for she had the very best of reasons for knowing that my anal orifice could contain anything of the gauge of his thick shaft without injury. Then she asked Abelard sarcastically if he had never taken a maidenhead before and what he meant by fumbling there with only three inches of cock stuck into me!

"'Charge into her like men,' she demanded, "until your four balls bang together under her rump!" Thus incited, they became desperate. Father Abelard lifted up my legs upon his arms, while Eustace supported me with his hands under my buttocks. Then they both reared back at the hips and plunged forward, burying their cocks in me. I screamed at this ultimate violation. I felt as if my belly and the entire lower half of my body were filled with two red-hot iron pokers. They fucked me heartily, reaming me entirely from back and front. The force of the shoves, especially from the rear, left me breathless—I could feel that huge cock buried deeply in my anal canal worming back and forth insistently. The one in front found smoother passage, but the outrageousness of the shoves from the head to the balls near drove me into unconsciousness. The two of them erupted together in a raging flood, so that my bottomhole and cunt absolutely overflowed with foaming cream, in the latter case considerably streaked with blood from my broken virginity. Now all this no doubt sounds very shocking to your ears, dear Auguste, but I did not altogether dislike it. No girl despises praise and flattery, and I certainly had enough of that. In addition, when the monks had recovered themselves a little, they kissed me rapturously, and promised me every indulgence that I liked. Father Abelard even said that if I would take the vows he would use all his influence for my advancement. As he shortly afterwards become a cardinal I have no doubt but that he was as good as his word, and that I owe my present position, which is most unusual at my young years, almost entirely to his interest and patronage.

"So you see, my darling boy, that some good may even come by a young lady suffering herself to be treated with what a first seems nothing but sheer lustful brutality." She took my hand in hers.

"What do you think of my story, Auguste?"

"I think," said I, "that I should have liked to have been there to see. But as it is I'm dreadfully excited, and I should like, if you have no objection—"

"What! You dear greedy boy!" she exclaimed.

"Well," I stammered out, hesitating, "what Father Eustace...did you like it? I think I should. I never have done yet, you know. May I try?"

"Oh, my bottomhole, you mean!" replied my aunt with great calmness. "Oh certainly. I dare say you'll enjoy it very much. I'll turn my rump towards you and stick it well out as I lie on my side. You can put your manly rod in as leisurely and lazily as you like." So saying she placed herself in the posture she described. I put the head of my cock to the starfish shaped aperture, amazed that my huge organ could find entrance in so small an opening. But I proceeded nonetheless, forcing it into her while she gasped and pushed back against me. This continued until the shaft was half-buried. The tightness was exquisite, and I revelled in the near painful sensation. Then I leaned forward and drove deeper with my weight until the length of the shaft found harbor. I began to work it in and out, drawing it out to the head and pushing it slowly in until it again fully disappeared. I increased the pace until it seemed I was fucking in near normal fashion and came within one or two additional strokes, copiously wetting the rearward portion of my companion. This being concluded to our mutual satisfaction, my beautiful bedfellow and I fell asleep in each others arms.

Early in the morning we were awakened by an elderly lay sister bringing in chocolate and biscuits. Not being in on the secret, she regarded me with some curiosity, and supposed that I was an innocent girl who had been unnaturally treated. She made some anxious inquiries after my health and offered her services to help me to dress. I thanked her, after which my aunt said that we weren't going to rise for an hour, that she would help her niece to dress, and we should require no assistance.

"The abominable prying old woman!" exclaimed Agatha. "But she has brought us this good chocolate, which, laced with a spoonful of brandy, will be an excellent restorative."

As we drank it, my aunt revealed to me a plot she proposed with my assistance to carry into execution against one of the nuns. This Sister Agnes was not only very devout herself, but unnecessarily rigid in her notion of propriety, correcting the slightest appearance of levity among the novices and the younger sisters, and threatening to inform the visiting monks of the slightest appearance of indecorum. Indeed, my aunt had discovered that she had really done so. Father Eustace told her of the matter as a good joke. But she was annoyed at having her province as Lady Abbess trespassed upon and had determined to get the girl, for she was little more, being barely twenty, into a snare of some sort. That way the squealer could no longer pride herself upon her propriety of conduct, and my aunt would be no longer troubled with her prudery and spying.

Agatha assured me that there was nothing disagreeable in the part she wanted me to play in the little scheme. The aforesaid Agnes was really a very fine, tall, dark-haired, slender girl, and if any ravishing or any less violent form of fucking had to be done, She was sure I would find it a very delightful occupation.

Her plan was this, to write a confidential note to Sister Agnes, complimenting her on her zeal for the purity of the convent, and the watchful eye she kept upon the younger sisters. Then she would mention the presence of her niece (meaning me), being fresh from the gaieties of Paris life, and expressing her dread lest I should be infecting or even corrupting the novices with descriptions of what I had heard or seen in the wicked world outside the convent walls.

She would therefore beg dear Sister Agnes to keep a sharp eye upon me. If she fancied that I had been too long in the company of any of the young ladies, she was to enter the room suddenly, as if by accident, and on the slightest appearance of improper familiarity, bring me instantly to her (the Mother Superior's) private apartment to be reprimanded. This note was written and sent with an appearance of secrecy to Agnes.

My instructions were to be as familiar as I pleased with Emilie, Adele, or Louise. "Only," said my dear aunt, "do reserve a little of your strength, in case I should require you to humble Agnes' pride."

"How shall I know Agnes when I see her?" I asked.

"By her demure and sanctified look," was the answer. "Besides, she never indulges in the slightest irregularity in her dress. She is in black, and the only luxury she indulges in is the finest black silk stockings. Perhaps, dear Auguste, before the day closes you will know more about those stockings than you do now. Mind you follow her with apparent reluctance, when she brings you to

45

me. Between fucking Emilie, Louise and Adele, you will surely manage to give her cause for doing so. So for the present, dearest Auguste, adieu!"

CHAPTER IV

After breakfast my aunt summoned Emilie, and gave me into her charge. She told her to introduce me to the pleasantest and best looking of the young ladies, and that we might amuse ourselves with embroidery or other similar work. And so she dismissed us, to the great delight of Emilie. Actually I'd been afraid that my aunt's rest and refreshment might have restored her lust to such an extent that I would have to service her once again. I was hoping to gather my strength for the benefit of the young ladies in whose company I planned to find amusement and gratification.

When we were in the corridor Emilie threw her arms around me and kissed me rapturously, saying how glad she was to see me.

"I hardly expected to see you looking so healthy after passing the night with our Lady Superior. How did you like your bed fellow? Was she very lusty?"

And so she rattled on until she had extracted from me an account of part of the night's amuse-

47

ments. The was thrilled as well to learn of our plans for dear Sister Agnes.

"Oh," Emilie exclaimed, "that will be really delightful. She is so prudish and sanctified and such an old maid, that I am glad to hear that the pride and formality will be taken out of her a little. I'll take very good care that if there is no impropriety going on when she visits our apartment, there very soon shall be. I think I can guess what your aunt intends to do. She will get Agnes safely into her chamber with you under pretense of hearing her complaints, and then with your assistance strap her down on the edge of the bed with a leg fastened to each of the foot posts. If she is placed in that convenient position, I hope you'll split her cunt up handsomely with your cock. If you don't, I'll never forgive you. And, speaking of bedrooms, I suppose there can be no impropriety in one young lady showing another her sleeping apartment," she laughed. "Perhaps you'll come and see what a nice little room I have got. It's close at hand."

I followed her into her snug little chamber, where her first action was to bolt the door. The second was to put her hand up my petticoats and grasp my tool which was already half-erect, while she kissed me and murmured some broken sentences in my ear to the effect that she had been dreaming of me all night. She had hoped that day before that I might have managed to ride her, but circumstances prevented it. She was afraid that similar circumstances might prove an obstacle today if I didn't seize the moment. She longed for me, she moaned. In fact, she begged and prayed me to fuck her as if it was the greatest boon Heaven or earth could grant her.

I was by no means indifferent to her entreaties. She evidently was passionately fond of me, and I was more than eager to fill her wishes. I thrust my hand up her petticoats as she had hers up mine and what I felt certainly urged me on. For the lips of her cunt were open; the moist tunnel was burning hot. Upon pushing my finger well into the interior, I felt her clitoris asserting itself like a little cock. My fingering procured the expected results; her canal became a slick and drippingly eager receptacle and my prick stood stiff as an iron bar. Without further delay I dragged her clothes up to her armpits, pushing her at the same time upon the edge of the bed. That done, I raised my own petticoats and presented my prick at the lightly-mossed lips of her cunt. I shoved into her at once, right up to the balls with my very first thrust. This produced a single exclamation of "Oh!" from the young lady, speedily stopped by my lips being pressed to hers and my tongue rolling into her mouth. I slowly withdrew my lance until the swollen head resided just within the juicy folds, then I leaned forward so as to clasp her heaving breasts while plunging in once again. I could feel my shaft scraping the tender inner membranes as I penetrated to the core of her belly. I began slowly thrusting with steady tempo, gradually increasing the length and force of the strokes. Eventually I was ramming into her like a man insane while she shrieked and squirmed and wriggled beneath me. My pent-up flood could no longer be restrained after another series of lunges and I released it with a satisfied groan. My cock, buried deeply in her pussy, jerked free its load of burning creme, thoroughly inundating Emilie's innards.

After we'd rested a bit, Emilie carefully wiped and dried my creme-coated tool. Then we hastened to arrange our dresses, after which we exited Emilie's room. "You know," she said. "I think you might manage to fuck Louise under the under pretense of its being some innocent little game you were playing with her. She not only has no experience, but she doesn't seem to have any ideas on the subject. She is totally ignorant, but I think you may open her eyes!"

"By opening her thighs I suppose," was my reply, at which she laughed. Together we entered the morning room that was occupied by some of the novices.

There were seated Adele, Louise, and a third party I didn't know, who seemed to be a lay sister instructing the young ladies in the mysteries of some sort of needlework. As we entered, she rose and retired and I was affectionately received by Adele and Louise.

After some talk of no consequence between a few girls in company, Adele began half in jest, half in earnest to ask more pointed questions. Adele, of course, was the novice who had the honor, experience and pleasure of passing the night as the bedfellow of the Mother Superior. She specifically wanted to know if Lady Agatha had fingered me, if she had made me finger her, if she had used a dildo on me, and if she had taken my maidenhead. To all of these questions I gave the best answers I could. I informed the girl that although my aunt did some fingering all the dildo work was of a new method that my aunt admired very much. Indeed, I said, I had the device on at that very moment. I must here remark that the experienced Emilie had fastened around my waist a belt which had a hole in the center, through which my cock and balls projected. This belt was buckled behind my rump and gave me the appearance of wearing a dildo. I don't think Adele would exactly have broken her heart with vexation if I had at once announced myself to be a young man, and proposed to fuck her on the spot! But with Louise it was necessary to use a little caution. Of course, both girls expressed a curiosity to see my novelty. Adele impudently proposed to take up my petticoats and inspect me at once. Louise more slyly hinted that if I would be so kind she would like to see what sort of a thing it was.

Emilie checked Adele's ardor by telling her that she already had experienced such pleasure and that she herself had been well fucked by Father Eustace in the course of her penance the previous day. The sly monkey did not say anything of the loving performance in which she had shared just half an hour before. Therefore it was only fair that both she and Adele should give the first chance to Louise, who had never had either a real cock or an imitation, and who could not begin her experience under better circumstances. For this Louise thanked her and timidly asked what she was expected to do?

"First of all, my love," replied Emilie in a dictatorial tone, "you must raise up your frock and your underclothing, so that Mademoiselle d'Ermonville can make complete investigation of your secret treasures. When he—er, she, I mean—has done so, it will be easier for her to operate upon you, and you will experience more pleasure than pain. We don't want this to be one of those cases where a dildo has been rudely or carelessly inserted, and the girl operated upon has suffered needless pain, and felt sore for two or three days afterwards."

"Certainly," chimed in Adele, "when Lady Agatha poked me with that dildo of hers I was obliged to use milk and water for two days afterwards. My poor tender little pussy was quite raw."

"Don't frighten Louise with your nonsense," interrupted Emilie severely. "I'll guarantee she'll not have to endure any such disagreeable consequences from our young friend's instrument. It's not like a coarsely made ordinary dildo. Come, child, lift up your petticoats and let Mademoiselle Augustine take your measure."

The blushing girl obeyed her, pulling up her shift and undergarments, disclosing an alabaster belly and thighs between which nestled her fuzz-bedewed little cunt in all its maiden purity. Upon my gently unfolding the orifice with my fingers, it resembled nothing so much as a rosebud first opening through dark

51

brown moss. Of course, this had the effect which Emilie had designed, for she knew right well that I should require some stimulant after my recent attack upon her. So under the influences of seeing, feeling and kissing the innocent Louise's sweet cunt, my cock began to assert its manly strength once again and rise to the occasion.

Just at this moment, Adele—who was half mad at witnessing performances which she wanted to share in, but could not—began peeping under my petticoats to see if the dildo was in good order and well strapped on. This made me rather nervous, as I feared a premature discovery. But glancing at Emilie and seeing her nod to me and smile I judged that even if Adele did guess at the truth it would be no great matter.

Our relative positions were thus: Louise stood with her legs apart, while Emilie held up her clothes, and soothed and caressed her. I, on my knees, was with my mouth and fingers preparing the pretty, velvet-lined sheath for the reception of my prick, when Adele crouched down between Louise's legs, and dragged up my petticoats. She amused herself with inspecting what she no doubt at first supposed to be my dildo. But the truth had to dawn on her. In the first place though the strap was there, a close observer could see that the "dildo" was not firmly connected with the strap. In the second place the elasticity, throbbing, and animal heat of a real cock are unmistakable, and cannot be counterfeited by an artificial means however ingenious. My ideas on this subject were confirmed by the lascivious girl, who proceeded to fondle and suck and then wrap her lips and tongue around my noble tool. I knew no girl would care about doing such with a mere toy. But however pleasing and flattering this performance may have felt, I became conscious that my intention with regard to Louise would be completely frustrated if this contin-

52

ued, and that the administration of a dose of warm cream in Adele's mouth would be but a poor apology for not taking her young friend's maidenhead. I accordingly thought it high time to proceed to business. I intimated as much to Emilie, who asked me in what position I would like the innocent victim of lust to be placed.

Looking around the room I could see nothing better than a low divan without back or sides. I suggested that if the sweet girl was laid down on that with a pillow under her rump, and that if Emilie on one side and Adele on the other would each hold up one of her legs, her position would be most satisfactory. This would enable me to get well into her with as little trouble as possible to herself, and with the utmost amount of gratification to me. Also that would afford the spectators a fair and full view of the entire proceedings from beginning to end. Louise lay down on her back, and drew her clothes up as high as they would go. That way there would be nothing intervening between my belly and hers. They held her legs up tolerably high, and as wide apart as a virgin's could well be pulled without hurting her.

As I made my own trifling preparations, Emilie whispered to me to unbuckle and let fall the dildo strap as it was of no further use for purpose of deception, and might encumber me and hurt Louise. I obeyed instantly.

"And now," said she, "if you think you have wetted her orifice with your tongue sufficiently, charge into her and good luck to you!"

I didn't need further urging than the sight of that enticing slit awaiting me. I reared back and buried the purpling head of my tool between her taut lips. The very first push I made elicited a scream from Louise. This elicited a laughing remark from Adele, who said, "I think we ought to wish 'good luck' to poor Louise instead of this young gentleman, for she'll be dreadfully sore after all this performance. Upon my word Emilie, I think we had better put a handkerchief or two between her rump and the divan or it will be all stained with sperm and blood." This they effected, though with some difficulty, for Louise really had not strength enough to raise her rump because of my vigorous pushes. I didn't mean to give her any unnecessary pain, but any one who has had the pleasure of snatching the maiden treasure of a fine, well-shaped, vigorous girl, just budding into womanhood, must be quite aware that it is not accomplished without occasioning some trouble and perhaps a little soreness to the gentlemen, and more or less pain and grief to the victim. In our case this was especially true—for not only was Louise naturally small and tight, but she had never been a participant in any of the amusements so much favored by the young ladies of the convent. She had never been dildoed—that was quite evident; and I don't think that she had ever been fingered.

I think that it was about the fifth or sixth heavy push that I broke down her barrier and got fairly into her. Louise faintly screamed and begged me to have mercy upon her and draw myself out of her. But while she was uttering these broken exclamations, she clasped me tightly around the neck and pressed her lips to mine. I didn't think it necessary to comply with her wishes further so I drew out about four inches, then plunged in again with renewed vigor up to the hilt of my weapon. Her sheath clasped my pulsing rod tightly, milking it with each piston-like stroke. Her protests faded into sighs of pleasure as I began the steady pumping motions designed to release her reservoir of pearly nectar and uncork my own stream of sparkling vintage. I forced myself deeper and deeper until our mounts fairly ground together, the hairs mingling and our bellies scraping. So constricted was her passage around my shaft that that three or four strokes were all that was required to bring me to the bursting point. I could feel the swell of my bursting cock-head as it filled with the rush of my boiling sperm. At the same time, Louise released a flow of warm fluid that fairly erupted from her nearly-filled slit and mixed with the blood of her broken maidenhead to ooze down her milky thighs. I exploded into her, spasming into her until I was left spent and lifeless.

As I lay prostrate on Louise's body, thinking with a sort of languid satisfaction of this being the first maidenhead that I had ever had the pleasure of enjoying, saucy Adele considered it an excellent opportunity to ascertain whether or not her suspicions as to my sex were correct. Accordingly, she commenced pulling my rump about in a most indecent manner, and very soon confirmed that my balls at any rate were fixtures.

"And I have no doubt," she said, addressing Emilie, "that the prick is equally genuine, as we shall find out when this young gentleman condescends to draw his sword out of the scabbard. Indeed, Emilie, I think we should pull him off that exhausted girl, for both for her sake and ours. Suppose someone were to come in? Indeed I'm surprised Sister Agnes has not been here long ago. She generally manages to intrude herself when any romping or fun is going on and either reports us for improper behavior or casts a chill over us by her prudish language and manners."

"Well," replied Emilie, "I not only expect her, but hope she will come in presently, but not quite yet. So I quite agree with you that we had better get our performers into a more decorous position, get their dresses and hair into something like order, and give them some refreshment. I dare say the gentleman wants it as well as the lady."

"Pray, Mademoiselle Emilie, when and how did you come to know the sex of this handsome young fellow?" asked Adele. "Was it revealed to you in a dream? A wet dream? Or did he himself reveal the fact to you in your waking moments when you had your petticoats up and your legs open? I don't know where of course, but perhaps in the corridor, or in the water-closet, or in your own bedroom? There now you're blushing. I declare I thought you had forgotten how to do so."

Emilie replied, laughing, "Never you mind, saucy girl, how I acquired my knowledge. But please, when Agnes makes her appearance, follow my lead, and back up what you see me and the so-called Mademoiselle d'Ermonville proposing, talking about, or doing with regard to her. Now let's give these used up turtledoves a glass of wine."

While they were conversing together, they had managed to get our dresses into something like order. We had hardly finished our refreshment when Sister Agnes entered and was received by the young ladies politely and kindly, if not affectionately.

I was duly and formally introduced as Mademoiselle d'Ermonville, and she immediately said, "Oh yes, I know! I had the honor of making the acquaintance of your mother, Mademoiselle. She is walking in the garden with Father Eustace. It shows a blessed disposition on her part to choose the society of the virtuous and good!"

Here Emilie began to cough, and I—to conceal my laughter—began to beg Sister Agnes to join me in taking a glass of wine. She replied that it was not her custom before noon but she would break her rules in order to welcome a stranger so estimable as Mademoiselle d'Ermonville. All this was very pleasant and decorous, and while it passed I had leisure to form my ideas of Sister Agnes as far as her outward appearance went.

She was tall, well shaped and decidedly good looking, but neither her face or her figure had that healthy plumpness of contour which is one of the most attractive features of girlhood and she was little more than a girl. Her face, too, was pale, though not unhealthily so. Altogether, I felt convinced that common report was right, and that Sister Agnes kept the vigils and fasts as prescribed by the church with the greatest strictness...too strictly perhaps for her health. Of course the natural result of such asceticism was that her temper was slightly soured, and that she looked with an angry eye on the rompings, playfulness, and other less pardonable amusements occasionally indulged in by the novices and the younger members of the sisterhood. Of this peculiarity the astute Emilie took advantage, as will be shortly narrated, to raise Agnes' anger to the desired point of her taking both Emilie and myself into the dreaded presence of the Lady Abbess of Ste. Claire.

CHAPTER V

"Tell me, sister Emilie, how have you been entertaining our guest?" asked Agnes after a short time.

"She has been entertaining us," was Emilie's reply. "She has been telling us about the young ladies, and the handsome men, and the imprisonments, and the executions, and the processions in the streets. They must be extraordinary, with handsome women completely naked, representing Goddesses of Reason, or something or other and all sorts of wonderful things."

"All most blasphemous and indecent," interposed Sister Agnes angrily. "I wonder that Mademoiselle d'Ermonville could not find more profitable subjects to talk about."

"Oh, let me assure you sister Agnes," said I, "I have been endeavoring to persuade these young ladies that in all my experience of the Court as it used to be, or of the present altered state of society, I have never met three such lovely girls as I have seen since I have visited the convent of Ste. Claire. And now indeed," said I looking at Agnes, "I may say four and not three."

"Your compliments are quite thrown away upon me, Mademoiselle," she gravely replied, "and I think you might be better employed than in turning the heads of these giddy girls with flattery and nonsense."

"Their heads, my dear Mademoiselle Agnes..." I said, "...bless your innocence, I've been looking at these legs as well! These three beauties had some dispute as to who of the three had the prettiest legs, and I have had some difficulty in deciding; perhaps you will assist me?"

At this indelicate proposal Agnes seemed struck dumb with horror, but on my giving a signal to Emilie and Adele they took the hint immediately and Louise followed their example, though with some hesitation. Each of them placed one of their little feet upon the divan which had just served as the altar for Louise's sacrifice; drawing up their petticoats they displayed their graceful legs. On these proceedings Agnes looked with a tremendous frown.

I suppose she thought that any interference on her part was useless, and was concocting an accusation to lay before the Superior. In the most impudent way I called her attention to the pretty show, remarking: "You see? It is not very easy to form a judgment or to give a preference where all three are so nearly perfect in their own particular way. Emilie's legs are the largest and show the most muscular development, while Louise's are very delicate and graceful. On the other hand, Adele, proud of her white thighs, has exhibited very good taste in wearing red silk stockings. The contrast between scarlet and white is very striking, indeed it is a pity that we have not two or three fine young gentlemen here to appreciate it!"

While I was making these impudent remarks I kept handling the limbs submitted for my inspection

59

in the most indecorous way. I didn't merely stroke the legs but proceeded well up the thick part of each girl's thighs. And because Adele was the only one of the three whom I had not fucked that morning, curiosity induced me to feel what sort of furry treasure she concealed. I did so, and gave her cunt a good rummaging with my forefinger, at which she giggled with delight.

At all this Agnes purpled and became very angry, chiefly towards Emilie, who she said had been long enough in the Convent to know that such indecencies were not permitted. She added that she would report us all to the Superior, so that the novices might be severely punished, and I might be sent away to carry my lascivious worldly practices elsewhere.

All this tended towards the object which Emilie and I had in view; but she, who was a devil for mischief, resolved to bring matters to a climax.

"Oh, Sister Agnes," she said, "you can't be so cruel. The fact is, Mademoiselle Augustine has the best shape of any girl in the nunnery, and is quite vexed when she hears anyone else praised. You have no idea what fine legs and thighs she has, and she is as proud of them notwithstanding her prudery as a young married lady is of a big belly."

"Talk of Adele's scarlet silks indeed! Why, Sister Agnes wears the finest black silk for the same purpose I suppose...to contrast with the whiteness of her thighs. Nobody ever sees them though, except by accident, but since we have a stranger among us who ought to see all the curiosities and ornaments of the Convent, I've no doubt but that she'll show them!"

To this Agnes returned an indignant rejoinder but in spite of her denial and her sanctity I could not help think that there was something in her manner which betrayed that she was not altogether insensible to Emilie's flattery.

Emilie approached Agnes, saying, "Don't be vexed with my nonsense, Sister Agnes, but let Mademoiselle

Augustine have one peep at your beautiful limbs!"
She threw her arms around her (clasping her so tight
that Agnes was nearly helpless), and exclaimed, "Now
Augustine, if you can't see what you want, you must
be a softy!" I took the hint at once, and lifted up
Agnes' clothes roughly enough, I dare say, and found
everything there just as Emilie had described it.

Now that I have time for reflection, I cannot help
thinking what an amount of vanity and flirtatiousness
may exist under a prudish exterior. If nobody was
intended to see Agnes' legs, why did she dress them in
the finest silk stockings, handsomely gartered half way
up to her thighs?

Well, I saw them at any rate, and so did Adele and
Louise, who were in raptures at my taking indecent
liberties with one whom they had been in the habit of
regarding as rather tyrannical in her notions of strictness. Their laughing remarks encouraged me to proceed further, and I began to pull Agnes' thighs open
and kiss her cunt. Her fair white bottom also came in
for its due share of my lascivious attention. In fact the
prudent and sanctified Sister Agnes was very near to
being fucked, when the door opened. The lay sister,
whom I had found in the room when I had first come
into it with Emilie, reentered to the great annoyance
of all of us, except Agnes, who, addressing her as
Sister Marie, demanded her immediate assistance in
conveying Emilie and myself before the Superior to be
punished for indecent and improper practices. The
elderly sister assented, but I thought it right to stand
upon my dignity, and told Agnes that I would be
happy to accompany her into the presence of my aunt,
but I would dispense with the company of the elderly
Sister Marie. I requested Marie to leave the apartments, which she, awed I suppose by the magical name
of my aunt, forthwith did. I turned around to Agnes,
and remarked with grave politeness, "Now, fair Sister,
if you have any communications to make to the Lady

Superior, and if my presence and that of our friend Emilie can be of service to you, we shall be happy to accompany you." This was taking the matter coolly and Agnes stared as if she hardly knew what to make of my assurance. But she had no choice; it was her own proposal to go to my aunt, and she could not shrink from it simply because we consented to accompany her. So she led the way. Emilie and I followed, laughing in our sleeves at the notion of the trap she was falling into.

We were duly ushered into my aunt's presence. She received all of us very graciously, saying, "Well, children, I hope you have been amusing yourselves. I like my young friends to enjoy themselves in any way consistent with propriety."

"I am sorry to have to say, Lady Mother," interrupted Agnes, "that I fear these two young ladies have not been amusing themselves with propriety."

"Indeed!" replied Lady Agatha, as if surprised. "Not Sister Emilie and my niece! Explain yourself, my daughter."

"I have merely to say," replied Agnes, "that your niece was examining the legs of Emilie, Adele and Louise, by way of deciding their rival claims to superiority."

"Well, well," said my aunt, "if that is true, there is no great harm in it! Young girls will be playful."

"Playful, Lady Agatha!" exclaimed Agnes. "Why your niece forgot ladylike propriety so far as to put her hands right up the young ladies' underclothes. I have no doubt she felt the lower part of their bodies. Indeed I am almost ashamed to say such a thing, but from Adele's exclamations and wrigglings about, I have no doubt Mademoiselle had managed to insert her finger in her private parts."

"Shocking! I can hardly believe it," said my aunt. "Is that all you have to tell me?"

"Well, my Lady," said Agnes, "I should think that

was enough. I don't wish to mention the indignities offered to myself."

"Proceed with your story, my daughter," said my aunt rather coldly. I could hardly help laughing, for I could plainly see that she was preparing in her mind to disbelieve the whole accusation.

Sister Agnes continued, "After my remonstrating with them to which they did not pay any attention, Emilie was wicked enough to fling her arms around me so as to render me helpless, and then your niece dragged up my clothes in the rudest and most violent manner. She then proceeded to violate the sanctity of my cunt and bottom. Indeed it seems a most extraordinary thing to say, but I felt as I suppose a girl must when she is being outraged by a young man. I could hardly conceive myself to be under the hands of a young lady!"

At this Emilie could not contain herself any longer, and burst into laughter! But she was immediately checked by my aunt, who preserved a face of laudable gravity, while she asked: "Did she hurt you, Sister Agnes?"

"Very much indeed," replied she, rather disposed to exaggerate her injuries.

"And what have you to say to this, young ladies?" said my aunt, addressing Emilie and me.

Of course I denied the whole affair from beginning to end; and Emilie went further, and asserted that Agnes had asked her to try and inveigle me into her chamber so that we three might have an indecent romp together.

At this brazen assertion Agnes held up her hands, calling upon the Virgin, blessed Ste. Claire and the Lord only knows how many angels to testify to her innocence and the falsehood of Emilie's statement, whereupon the Lady Abbess remarked that she had a difficult task to impose justice on us, for the assertions on both sides were so positive and strong.

"However, Agnes," she continued, "there is one thing that can be proved. If you have been hurt as you say, you must exhibit some marks of it. I am quite experienced enough to perceive the slightest irritation on such a tender spot. You may depend upon it that if I could find the slightest proof of the truth of your statement, the misbehaviors and falsehood of these girls shall be punished most severely." This my aunt announced with a most austere air. Then she told Agnes to seat herself on the edge of the bed, and prepare for a short examination.

Agnes obeyed at once. We were then requested to place ourselves one on each side, and hold up her legs, while the Lady Abbess investigated the state of her cunt so as to ascertain the truth of her statement.

As may have been anticipated, the Abbess could discover no signs whatever of rough usage. Indeed there were none; for the kissing and very slight fingering which I had administered to the virtuous Agnes had not disordered her pink little mossy nest in the slightest degree.

Lady Agnes, after pulling the taut lips open and peering within, declared her belief that the whole accusation was false, and decreed that Agnes should be punished. So, in spite of her vehement protestations, my aunt handed to Emilie and me a velvet covered strap and buckle, directing each of us to strap one of Agnes' legs under the knee to one of the bedposts. Then the question arose as to the punishment due to a sister nun who had maligned two young ladies and told falsehoods. My aunt pretended to insist upon her being flogged, but I begged for mercy, saying to my aunt that it was a pity such a lovely white rump should be disfigured by the lash. Emilie also suggested something less severe. At last she appeared to yield to our entreaties, saying that as we were the wronged parties, in being improperly accused, we should deal out the punishment. My idea was that, as

Agnes had accused me of fingering her I should take any liberties I liked with her in real earnest. Emilie, by way of furthering my intention, suggested a dildo.

My aunt told us that we might do as we liked with her, while Agnes begged for mercy. I told the poor girl in a half whisper that we were not going to flog her, or even to hurt her, and that if she would have a few minutes patience, we would release her legs from their position, if that was painful to her. By this it is easily comprehended that in two minutes I planned to have my cock into her nearly as high as her kidneys, and that I would just as soon have her fine silk-clad legs doubled across my back, instead of fastened up to the bedposts; but until then I wasn't going to forego the great advantage I had. For Agnes lay perfectly helpless, with her bottom well lifted up, and her thighs stretched so far apart that her pert little cunt was actually forced open.

All that I needed was a little ointment, with which I moistened her gaping orifice, while my kind aunt did the same for my throbbing cock. Emilie employed herself in tying my petticoats up to my armpits with a silk sash. Then I asked my assistants to raise Agnes' head with a pillow, for I like kissing a pretty girl's mouth, particularly during the few last rapturous strokes. Then, while my victim would be so employed, kissing me, I liked to ram my well-oiled prick into her burning parts.

It was to be the second maidenhead that lucky red-domed gentleman had visited that same day!

Also, as the position of her buttocks were extremely favorable, I passed one hand under her rump. I began by fingering the puckered neighboring orifice and obtained a much greater degree of liveliness and elasticity from her wriggling bottom than I otherwise should have enjoyed.

A pretense of piety and a sanctimonious demeanor do not always mean a girl is therefore a virgin; indeed very often when a young lady has allowed her passions to get the better of her, and has parted with her treasure to a forward lover, or has lost it by violence, she pretends to be a prude and puritan. However, this was obviously not the case with Agnes. I felt my probing cock-head encounter her obstruction, but it was hardly a barrier to my ravaging thruster. I reared back slightly at the hips and pushed forward slowly, not wishing to cause Agnes undue pain. As she didn't seem to experience any discomfort, I repeated the motion more forcefully, enjoying the sensation elicited by the passage of my shaft in her smooth canal.

I found my way into Agnes' body after the second or third thrust, and that without eliciting a scream. To my delight I perceived that whereas dear little Louise felt too much pain to appreciate my thrusts and raptures, or to reciprocate the creamy flood which I injected into her, my present victim, on the contrary, was disposed to do both, as I soon perceived from her gaspings, kissings, and wrigglings. So, I signed to my attendants to unfasten her legs. As I anticipated, she immediately folded them across my naked loins and around my back, lifting her rump clean off the bed. As she did so, she met a tremendous shove of my prick, nearly half way. I was buried to the balls in her flowing cunt, my thick shaft stretching her pussy lips to the utmost.

At length the mutual loving discharge took place. I deluged the interior of her canal with warm sperm oil that shot from my engorged cock head in milky gouts, while she saturated my noble prick even to the twitching sac, and the curly brown hair that covered its roots.

As we lay quiet face to face, she breathlessly whispered to me, "Oh, how I love you! You are a young man, are you not?"

I smiled assent, then she continued, "If you love me and have found any pleasure in what you have been doing, or value the virginity you have just robbed me of, please set me right with your aunt, and do me the justice to say that I am innocent of what you and Emilie have accused me."

This I readily promised to do. All this passed unheard by my Lady Abbess, and Sister Emilie, who were amusing themselves by stroking and handling my balls, pumping my flaccid shaft in an attempt to restore it to its firm and proud state, patting and slapping my buttocks, and cramming their fingers up my rump. In fact, although I had done my duty to my aunt the night before, and Emilie's cunt could hardly have been dry since my attack upon her in the morning, they both seemed mad with lust, as if they hadn't been fucked for a fortnight!

I put a stop to their lascivious liberties with my person by raising my body and releasing Agnes, who blushed deeply as she rose, and prepared to adjust her disordered dress.

"Stop a little," exclaimed Lady Agatha. "Emilie and I will wipe you dry, and make you comfortable."

"How did you like it? Ha! A little blood I see, not much. That was a fine shove which broke through your maidenhead, was it not?"

Thus laughing and making fun of what to poor Agnes was really a serious transaction, they wiped her pouting cunt lips from which oozed the thick fluid of our passion and made her as comfortable as she could reasonably expect to be.

But when Agnes began to solemnly protest her innocence, and called upon me to confirm it, my aunt cut her short with, "Bah, we know all about it, my dear. It was all a planned thing between me, Emilie and my nephew here, Monsieur Auguste d'Ermonville, to whom I beg to introduce you, although I think he has managed to introduce himself already and that in a very appropriate manner."

And again she laughed merrily, then continued,

"Mind, Agnes," she said, "that whatever has taken place in this room is as sacredly secret as if it had never been. You must not even reveal it to your confessor."

This Agnes cheerfully promised.

"And now," said my aunt, "as we have pretty well used up our young gentleman between us, and cannot expect more gratification from him, we will amuse ourselves with a glass of champagne and some chocolates and we will exchange some stories to amuse ourselves."

While she was providing the refreshments, I sat down on the sofa and drew Agnes on my knee. The feel of her bare bottom on my lap sent a tingle of lust and excitement through me.

Thus comfortably situated, I was prepared for anything that was forthcoming in the way of amusements, or story telling, or any other rational or agreeable amusements. Agnes' position seemed to provoke the jealously of both the other ladies and Emilie said that she thought it was her turn now. My aunt merely said, "Well, Auguste, I suppose your maxim is last come first served. Anyway, Agnes will not be fit to be fucked again for forty-eight hours, that's one comfort!"

"Nor will Louise, that's another comfort," exclaimed Emilie, with great satisfaction.

"What? Two maidenheads in the course of one morning?" laughed my aunt. "Upon my word, my dear nephew, you are playing the bull among my young heifers! Call in Adele and Louise, my dear Emilie. The latter must want some refreshment; and if the former wants anything else, I'll call in Father Eustace. Or if, as is likely enough, he is worn out with his attentions to my sister, Adele, must be satisfied with a dildo!"

Upon this the four girls cast lots, and the lot fell upon Louise, the youngest, and most inexperienced of the four.

She began by saying that she feared that she would be unable to amuse us, that she really was perfectly ignorant of everything. But on being cross-examined by my sagacious aunt, she confessed to having seen something of which she could tell, though she could hardly call it amusing.

"Leave us be the judge of that," said the Abbess. "Tell us all about it."

Louise proceeded thus: "About two years ago on the death of my mamma, my father sent me into the country to visit his mother, a venerable lady, who lived in great seclusion. He thought that the change of air and scene would be beneficial to me. Accordingly, accompanied by my own governess—a handsome but very strict middle-aged lady of thirty—I duly made my appearance at the chateau of Madame de Fleury. I was most kindly received by her, but my pleasure was somewhat damped when I noticed her nephew—a most extraordinary man of deficient mental capabilities who was in appearance much like an ape. He was short and heavily built; his brow was almost like a gorilla; and he was covered with thick, coarse hair. What's more he never spoke, but communicated with bestial grunts and groans. She assured me that he was perfectly tame, and quite harmless, and that I must learn to be familiar with him, as he had been, for many years the only companion and amusement of a lonely old woman. So I did my best to get rid of my fears; indeed Sylvian—for that was his name—was the only object of which I had any reasonable dread, and that I got over with the assistance of my strong-minded governess who did not seem to have any dread of him at all, but rather seemed to like him. She was so fond, she said, of studying human nature, so similar to that of the beast. Now I knew nothing of nature, much less of wickedness, but at least even I in my ignorance began to think it rather extraordinary that this ape-like man should begin to follow Madam Herbelot around the house and grounds, instead of remaining with his mistress, as was his former custom.

"At first I fancied that it was only on account of the delicacies and sweets that she used to feed him. But I soon observed certain peculiarities. I noticed that when my governess, Madam Herbelot came into the room, and particularly if she approached him, a huge bulge would appear in the front of poor Sylvian's trousers.

"But never mind that! While Madame de Fleury was in the room, my governess pretended never to show any interest in Mr. Chimpanzee, as I called him, whether he exhibited any animal propensities or not. But one day even my Grandmother, who was partially blind, could not help noticing the state of lust the poor fellow had worked himself into, and she remarked to my governess: 'It is a pity that I cannot get a female companion for poor Sylvian, the dear creature is wearing himself out.' I may remark here that neither my relative or my governess were aware of my presence in the room, for I sat in an embrasure shrouded by the curtain, out of which, as I peeped, I beheld this ugly caricature of a man, grasping what I suppose I must call his cock through his very trousers with one hand while he worked it quickly up and down. At this sight my grandmother looked with something like sorrow and pity. Madam Herbelot observed it with interest and curiosity. It was a great pity, continued my grandmother in a musing tone, as she looked at the man-beast, who had now concluded his performance. If he goes on frigging himself in this way, he'll kill himself. She wondered if she could find a peasant girl who for a crown or two would let him do what he liked with her.

"'Would not that get her large with an idiot-child, my dear Madame de Fleury?' inquired my governess.

"'It needn't do anything of the sort,' replied my grandmother dictatorially. 'If such should be the case I should take care of the progeny, but it need not be so; for if she kneels down on all fours with her rump uppermost, there is no fear of his producing any result upon her; or indeed for that matter he might fancy shoving his cock into her rumphole itself, perhaps better than the other orifice: it would be much the same to her, and anything to please him, poor fellow!'

I wondered considerably at the interest exhibited by my aged relative for this hideous creature; but I suppose people with little family, and rarely seeing their friends or acquaintances, must fix their affections on something. It seemed, though, that my Grandma's remarks had made considerable impression upon the mind of my governess. One strange circumstance I must mention: Sylvian was locked in at night to prevent his wandering around the house; his apartment, I dared not call it a den, was situated close to Madame's sitting room.

"Entering early one morning to get a book which I had left there on the previous evening, I heard Sylvian grunting as if much excited. On my peeping slightly to see what was the matter, I saw my respected governess holding up her petticoats with her left hand, so as to display her thighs, her belly, her cunt, and all in fact that I had always been taught that a woman should keep concealed. With her right hand she grasped Sylvian's huge stiff red rod and worked it up and down until I thought the man would go mad with his unquenched lust and inability to get at what he wanted, which was of course her private parts displayed purposely to excite him. However, this kind of thing could not last long, and in a minute or two some milky fluid jerked out of his cock so far as to fall in one of Madame's slippers as she stood close opposite to him. Then the brute sank down on the floor; and I made a hasty and noiseless retreat not wishing to disturb my governess in her studies of biology. But it seemed that two days afterwards she was pursuing these studies with unabated vigor, for as I was out in the garden reading in one of the numerous arbors, my chambermaid Annette, who hated Madame Herbelot, called to me in a whisper, 'Mademoiselle,' and beckoned me to follow her. This I did with some curiosity.

"She led the way to a secluded part of the garden where there was also an arbor such as I had left, but overgrown and neglected. Arriving here, Annette put her finger to her lips and peeped through the mass of foliage. I cautiously followed her example, and soon observed my mistress, the discreet Madam Herbelot, on her hands and knees like some four-footed animal, sticking out her posteriors for the benefit of Monsieur Sylvian, who was certainly availing himself of his position with all the delight and enjoyment which his beastly ingenuity could devise. One thing Annette and I both noticed, that perhaps on account of the conversation which I had overheard between my grandmother and my governess, the latter had prudence enough even in the height of her unnatural lust to take some precautions. Or maybe it was that the man-beast himself preferred that mode of operation—either are likely—at any rate, one thing is certain that he had his cock shoved up my governess' rumphole as far as he could go, and actually repeated his performance twice while we were looking at them. At last he withdrew his dripping pole, and Annette and I retired. She whispered to me, 'She won't be able to walk tomorrow, Miss, but she shall ride, for I'll tell Madam de Fleury and get her sent home.' And to make an end of my long story, so she did."

CHAPTER VI

"Your story, my dear Louise, comes to rather an abrupt termination," remarked the Abbess. "You certainly seem to have had a very remarkable experience for an innocent girl, and have told us a very nice story; but I think you should make a finish to it. For instance, what reason did Madame de Fleury give for sending your governess away? And what did the monkey-man, Sylvian, if that was his name, do without his lady friend? And did your grandmother carry out her intention of getting a peasant girl into the chateau for his benefit?"

"I was afraid of becoming tedious, madame," replied the pretty novice, "but I can tell you something of what you wish to know, if it will give you any satisfaction. I learned from Annette that there had been quite a scene between Madame Herbelot and the old lady, the former declaring that it was only the account which Madame de Fleury had given her of her nephew's propensities and wants that had induced her to undertake an interest in him, and to extend her research into biology in that direction.

"Which ended in the baboon extending his researches into her rump," said my aunt, at which interruption we all laughed.

"But," continued Louise, "my grandmother told her, that although she herself was extremely practical, and had no objection to her amusing herself in her own way, especially since it gratified dear Sylvian, she thought that Madame Herbelot had devoted far too much time to such pursuits.

"And so they parted; my governess left ostensibly due to ill health. What is more, to my astonishment, my grandmother did not get into the chateau for her unnatural purpose any mere poor degraded girl.

"She got in a fine, well-shaped, buxom lass. She was very curious to find out what the result would be of a thorough copulation between her pathetic charge, and a pure healthy girl who naturally wanted fucking. But she was disappointed in her expectations, as you will shortly hear. It was not that Sylvian had not every chance; for Marie—that was her name—was well paid, fed and clothed, and was expected to fulfill her part of the contract...and so she did. Indeed my grandmother took care of that, for she very seldom permitted her interesting pair of breeding animals out of her sight. For instance, I might be sitting in her room reading to her, Marie sitting at needle-work or knitting at a respectful distance, while the man-beast was amusing himself in the apartment, cracking nuts or eating cakes. All of a sudden Madame would cry, 'Marie, my child, prepare yourself, I see my nephew is getting excited,' which meant that the fellow having fairly been apprenticed in the luxuries of a woman's private parts, began to have constant cock stands. On seeing this Marie began to show him immediate attention.

"Indeed I fancy that the dear old lady, though long past that sort of excitement herself, did feel something beyond mere ordinary amusement in witnessing the performances of these two and would call out to the poor girl when the beast was preparing for the attack, "Quick, Marie! Take up your clothes and get down on your hands and knees. I think dear Sylvian will prefer it that way this morning." Or perhaps it would be, "Stand up right before him and let us see him do it that way!"

"Pray," here interrupted the Abbess, "did your grandmother allow you to remain in the room while these strange proceedings were going on?"

"She did indeed, Madame," replied Louise, "for she was one of the haughtiest of aristocrats, and regraded her peasantry as just so many animals. I'm sure that she did not consider Marie, who was a good looking, plump, fat rumped, white thighed girl as one bit better than the ugly brute to which she was induced for pay to prostitute her girlish body. And as for my being in the room, she regarded it as a matter of no more concern than if one of her favorite dogs got fast into a pretty bitch in our presence. When this occurred, as it often did, Madame would survey the proceedings through her spectacles, and indulge in prognostications as to what sort of a litter was likely to be the result, just as she used to reflect on what sort of a production Marie would bring into the world after being fucked by the dumb brute. But such abominable expectations were not fulfilled, and I was glad of it. As I said, she came to be disappointed in this way: Connected with the chateau, Madame de Fleury had a very considerable farm, with, of course, its usual complement of servants, ploughmen, carters, herdsmen, and so on. Annette had a more than casual liking for a handsome young fellow who was the head of the cattle department. Accordingly one morning we were crossing the yard, when whom should we meet but this very Robert, who was leading by the halter a beautiful white heifer.

"'Good morning Miss Annette,' said he.

"'Good morning, Master Impudence!' she replied. 'Where are you going to with that pretty creature?'

"'She is going to get what would do you a great deal of good, and what I should like to give you,' said he.

"'Pray what's that?' asked Annette.

"'Come and see,' was the brief answer.

"So, as we had nothing better to do, and as idleness is the mother of all mischief, we followed him to a large stable at the far corner of the yard where I knew, but had not seen, that a large and valuable, but very fierce bull was kept for breeding purposes.

"Robert ushered us into the well kept stable, telling us not to be afraid, that there was plenty of room, that the bull was always fastened with a ring through his nose, and that he had his young assistant Jean in the stable.

"But as we entered, we not only saw Jean there, but Marie also. Upon my expressing my surprise, she apologized, but said that the stinking brute, for this was the disrespectful way in which she spoke of Monsieur Sylvian, was ill—that he had over-fucked himself, or over-drank himself, so that she came out to enjoy the fresh air and to see Jean, her cousin.

"I begged her to stay and not to go away, on my account.

"Robert said, 'Oh! Please Mademoiselle, permit her to stay for Jean's sake. I will take care of Annette, and I wish there was some handsome young viscount here to entertain your ladyship!'

"I wondered what on earth he meant; but my attention became speedily absorbed in what he and Jean were doing. The first thing Jean did was to fasten the heifer by the head in one of the large roomy stalls the stable contained, putting two or three strong posts or cross bars from that appropriated to the bull. Next Robert led out the magnificent beast, while Jean shook out two trusses of straw on the floor where he had been standing, muttering something about clean and dry for the ladies to stand on, but I found out afterwards that the straw was to serve other purposes besides standing on, but I will not anticipate. No sooner was the majestic bull introduced to the young heifer, than Jean fastened down behind them two heavy wooden bars; thus we were in safety outside, but Robert remained inside with the animal to Annette's great distress, who begged him to come out or the bull would kill him! Robert cooly replied that the bull had something else to do at present, and that he would come out as soon as he had done his duty, in less than a minute.

"By this time I partly guessed what all these proceeding would lead to. As for Annette I thought she knew from the first.

"But I was surprised when I saw the stupendous animal-cock erected by the bull, when he proceeded to mount the heifer. Imagine, young ladies if you can, a large carrot at least a yard long, with a huge pair of white dangling balls, each apparently as large as those balloons we sometimes see little boys with in the street. It now seemed that it was Robert's business to guide this huge machine to its destination—a most unnecessary proceeding it seemed to me, or else how does the animal manage to effect his purpose when in the wild.

But after he inserted the end of the bull's rod in the bonny heifer's open cunt, the poor creature absolutely shrinking and cringing under the enormous weight and tremendous shoves of the monstrous brute on top of her, Robert slipped out under the bars and stood contemplating the spectacle with one arm around Annette's waist, while he whispered something to her; she seemed very much excited, and said something about Mademoiselle.

"'Oh, You'll excuse us won't you, Mademoiselle de Fleury?' said Robert. "You see young men and young girls too, get excited by such a pretty scene as this. Annette and I are old sweethearts and Jean will take care of Marie.' I told them not to mind me. But my remark was unnecessary as far as Jean and Marie were concerned, for that stout youth had already got his cousin's petticoats up and his own breeches down. With one hand he rammed under her cunt and with the other he forced her backwards among the clean straw.

"Annette was treated more delicately. She was dressed neatly and even elegantly, and had no notion of being thrust backwards, and having her neat frock and underclothing disarranged. Bidding her lover wait a moment, she spread her shawl on the straw, to prevent its scratching her fair rump, I suppose, and then neatly and tidily gathering up her clothes, she seated herself with her back and shoulders supported by another truss, and opened her thighs wide and put her knees up. Then with a smile she invited Robert to come on, an invitation which he was by no means slow in accepting. He had been taking his breeches down in the meantime and gathering up his shirt, and his noble cock stood forth in all its naked majesty! Depend upon it, my dear girls, that there is nothing in nature equal to a healthy man's standing prick; there are all shapes and all sizes; some are thick, some are slender, some are short or long and thick, but they are all good in their way. Perhaps it seems somewhat presumptuous in me to talk to you in this way, especially as I was virginal until this morning, when naughty Auguste, who I don't doubt is now fingering Sister Agnes' cunt, robbed me of my maidenhead, hurt me and made me bleed. But still you see, Lady Agatha, I have seen what every girl has not seen.

Now Sylvian's prick was an uncommonly large and thick instrument, and half again as large as Robert's. But Robert's cock, about nine inches long, of a delicate light brown in color, well fringed at the root with dark hair, the end like a scarlet egg, was one of the finest objects I had ever seen, and quite worthy of the honor of admission into Annette's pretty little cunt. How the worthy Robert was to shove himself into that little orifice without splitting it open and spoiling my attendant I could not at first perceive. But it is my private belief that he had plumbed that territory before, and knew the way in. At any rate if he had not been, somebody or something else had, for there was no screaming, no begging for mercy, no bleeding—nothing in fact at all of what I was expecting. Robert exhibited very great judgment and good taste even in the height of his lascivious delight, for he consulted Annette's feelings by asking her, 'Are you nearly ready darling?' The only reply she made was dragging his face down to hers until their mouths seemed glued together, and twining her well-shaped legs around his loins as if she meant to break his back. With this Robert began to drive his cock into her pouting pussy with a force and power to which his former efforts were a trifle. There was some convulsive heaving and wriggling of Annette's posteriors, then Robert shoved his weapon in up to the balls, and sank down quietly, letting it remain there, while the girl gasped for breath.

"I had been so anxiously watching the pleasure of my chambermaid and her lover, that I had not paid much attention to Jean and Marie, who were only a couple of yards off in another part of the stall. But with regard to them, I could easily perceive that Jean had not treated Marie with the same delicacy with which Robert behaved to Annette. On the contrary he must have charged into her poor cunt most recklessly, merely for the satisfaction of his own lust; after satisfying himself, which he apparently managed to do in about a minute, he had recovered himself very quickly, for while Robert and Annette were yet lying languidly in each other's arms. The young lad was turning his cousin over on her hands and knees, proposing to have his second fuck rump uppermost. Of course, as Marie seemed to like her cousin and enjoy his fucking in the way he pleased, I could not blame him. But their new position produced an effect I did not anticipate. Madame knows very well, and the most innocent of all young ladies, can understand, that the posterior style and posture I have described exposes the whole person of both actor and actress in the plainest manner. It exhibits every shove on the part of the youth and every wriggle on the part of the girl's rump. In this instance it was so to the fullest extent.

"Robert lay lazily on Annette's plump bosom, and hearing rustling in the straw raised his head, and seeing what was going on hinted to his sweetheart to draw her attention that way. 'He has a very fine cock for a lad of his age,' remarked Robert in a critical sort of way!

"'Yes,' replied Annette, 'and she is not a bad sort of girl for a peasant girl; well-shaped buttocks and thighs and two very nice little holes, considering the beastly work with Sylvian she has had to go through lately. I do so hope that Jean will get her with ch-child: it will be be-better than a l-l-litter of m-m-monkeys, at any r-a-a-t-e.''

I wondered what on earth made Annette begin to stutter and stammer, and gasp for breath as she was speaking. Turning my gaze from the dog-fucking couple, I perceived that Monsieur Robert, who had never withdrawn his weapon from its warmly moistened sheath, was beginning to recover himself, and was plunging in and out slowly, and evidently very effectually. His expanding flesh-pole filled Annette's eager canal, stretching the tender lips and plumbing the inner reaches until his balls slapped her upturned buttocks with the ferocity of his thrusts.

"This couple was so very quiet and exhibited so much propriety that I was not afraid to ask Annette if she liked it, and whether such a great thing shoved into her body did not hurt her. She answered in broken sentences that it was most delicious, and that she felt the fiery throbbing tip of Robert's prick tickling her kidneys.

"Now if you want to know if these proceedings excited me, I must candidly reply that they did. Though I did not know the meaning of my own emotions, I was aware of a strange feeling coming over me, and almost fainting, I leaned against one of the posts in the stable for support. I stood with my legs somewhat apart, and involuntarily emitted a small quantity of some liquor or other from my secret parts—quite enough to moisten my chemise, spot my stockings in two or three places, and even drop on the ground between my legs.

"But I felt much relieved by this evacuation, and as Annette had by this time got as much poking as was good for her, we prepared to depart. I assured the happy couples that I would not betray their secrets, and Robert hoped that some day I might find a worthy young gentleman to give me similar pleasure. But I am afraid Lady Mother, that I am making too long a story and will weary you and these girls, permit me therefore to conclude.

"Very shortly after the interesting events which I have just related, my father summoned me home. As Annette expressed a wish to remain and marry Robert, I persuaded my father to give them a little money so as to enable them to take a small farm in the neighborhood. And it was from Annette, on the occasion of a visit she made to Paris that I heard the result of that which I witnessed at the Chateau de Fleury. It seems that Marie had the prudence to hoard her disagreeably earned wages, and it was well that she did so, for my grandmother's mind was so set on seeing the product of Sylvian's loins that the poor girl had to undergo every day and sometimes twice and three times the lustful embraces of the filthy brute. But even there, good came out of evil; for she told Annette, that if it had not been for the man-ape being equally pleased with her rump hole as with her cunt, she believed he would have fucked her into a decline. As it was she became pregnant and began to get very heavy, to the great delight of the scientific old lady.

While Madame was in this temper, Marie by Annette's advice got from her all the money, cast off dresses, and other presents that she could coax or wheedle out of the old lady. For Annete guessed how the affair would terminate, and knew what a tremendous storm would ensue. Well the girl delivered, of course, to the wrath and disappointment of Madame de Fleury. Why? The baby was not a curiosity but a fine baby boy, very much like its father, as it turned out. So out of the house Marie was sent packing; but thanks to her own care and Annette's advice, she had more money and clothes than any peasant girl in the district, or indeed most farmers' daughters in the neighborhood. Jean was discharged by his mistress, married Marie, and as man and wife they entered Robert's service as farm servants. Madame de Fleury died. As for Sylvian, little was heard of him, though Annette believed he was sent away, not to be seen again. So there is the end of my story, and I sincerely hope I have not tired you all by its tedious length."

We all hastened to assure the dear little girl that such was far from being the case, and the Abbess in particular remarked that she felt quite surprised that such an innocent inexperienced girl as Louise should have seen such extraordinary incidents and relate such an interesting story.

She then intimated to her that she was at liberty to call upon any one of the rest of the young ladies to contribute their share to the general amusement. After a little consideration, Louise selected Emilie, giving as her reason that she thought Emilie would be the most likely to tell about something that she had felt, whereas Louise could only tell what she had seen. To this Emilie laughingly assented. She commenced her story thus.

"Although my mother was left a tolerable fortune on the death of my father, she was by no means what is generally termed rich; still she liked to have everything about her in good style—house, furniture, carriage and servants.

"One thing she was very particular about, that the servants, male and female, who closely attended to her, should be good looking and well dressed. She did not object to giving high wages and she would overlook a little idleness or carelessness...but appearance was everything. Consequently, no one in the household felt much astonished when we learned Pierre Morin, the groom of the chambers, who was both stupid and ugly, though honest enough, had received his discharge. Albert, who was head page and her footman was promoted, and my mother's steward and housekeeper received orders to look out for a suitable ladies' page.

"In due time a youth made his appearance, highly recommended by the housekeeper, who informed my mother that he had good blood in his veins. What's more, the housekeeper was likely enough to know all about it, as I afterwards had the strongest reasons for believing him to be her natural son. Be that as it may, the youth was taken into the situation, and speedily became a great favorite with my mother, too much of a favorite I might have thought had I been older and more experienced. He certainly was uncommonly handsome, and I soon began to feel an interest in him on my own account.

"It was Victor's duty—that was his name—to wait in the anteroom to be ready at my mother's call. But as he was closely on duty all day she never took him out with her at night when she was going to a ball, the theatre, or a masquerade—for this she had regular carriage attendants. As for me, my mother did not consider me old enough to go into society, and I was left to amuse myself in the best manner I could when she was out. Now, though Master Victor had no business to be lounging about the boudoirs and antechambers during my mother's absence, he constantly was there, sometimes under pretence of cleaning and arranging things to rights, and sometimes pretending that he was in attendance on me. I believe that the housekeeper approved of his actions, and used to have rich chocolates made to serve with sweetmeats for him to bring up to me, to cloak his designs. After a little, when he became bolder, and I more familiar, he used to tell me stories of the world, not always of the most delicate character. One time for instance, he told of how a certain young Vicomte had been found by his mother on the sofa with his sister's governess between him and the cushions and his cock buried deeply in her yawning cunt.

"Though I did not altogether understand these stories, they were not without effect upon me. The young fellow then used to show me pictures, which without being absolutely indelicate, had a slight tendency in that direction.

"One evening, when my mother had gone to a masquerade and did not intend returning until three or four o'clock in the morning, Master Victor had made himself more than usually entertaining. He had shown me plenty of pictures and told me lots of amusing stories, and I'm ashamed to say I was getting rather fond of him. As he was pulling some pictures out of his pockets, there fell on the floor what seemed either a large pocket book or a small portfolio. This I grabbed and tried to open. He smiled at my efforts and said the book was not intended to be opened by everybody, that there were secrets in it, and so on. All this raised my girlish curiosity, and I insisted on knowing and seeing the contents of the book.

"'Very well then, the picture represent a series of dramatic scenes, enacted by a young lady and gentleman in private,' he said. 'Amateur theatricals, with no spectators.' I insisted upon seeing the pictures immediately. He complied, sitting himself close beside me on the sofa, and exhibited the pictures one by one. The book opened with a concealed spring, a curious and unnecessary precaution I thought, for there was nothing in the slightest degree improper in the first two or three pictures. Then I speedily altered my opinion. I cannot go over all the pictures one by one, but I might mention that the first represented lovemaking between a young lady and gentlemen; showing them walking with their arms around each other's waist in a garden, he kneeling at her feet as she sat in an arbor, kissing very sedately; but when Master Victor, presuming on my indulgence, suggested that we should imitate the scenes before us, I only laughed and told him not to be impudent.

"This apparently he took for consent, for he knelt by my side and dragged my right arm around his neck and wound his left arm around my waist. This was decidedly improper conduct by a page towards the daughter of the house. But it did not end there; for the next picture represented the young lover in a more forward character. He had got his breeches down and his right hand up the young lady's petticoats, while her person was most indecently exposed. The sight of this picture struck me with shame, and yet somehow or other I could not keep my eyes from it. This I don't doubt was perceived by the saucy page, who insinuated his hand up my petticoats and began to finger my untried and lightly-mossed cunt. I ought, I suppose, to have risen and rang the bell, or screamed out for assistance; but for the life of me I could not do either. He got his forefinger well into me, past the clutching lips and deep in my cave, and began to excite me. As I turned over the next leaf of the seductive book, I happened to look down and saw that my young friend had got his stiff prick exposed and ready. He was long and thin and venous and was capped with a plum-like helmet with a slit in its end that seemed almost to smile at me. Not that my ideas were altogether formed on the subject then, but I was certainly very angry and rather frightened. But his handsome face was turned up to mine with such a passionate and imploring air that I felt softened and irresolute, and to hide my confusion I turned my eyes to the picture I had just looked over. And what a picture! It represented the lover as having got on so well in his love-making and seductive arts, that he was on the verge of the fuck, and the young lady was shown with her legs up his arms, and her thighs wide open, while his red-headed prick was seeking admission at her private entrance. The sight of this pretty picture completed my confusion, and I hardly knew what I was doing. Victor quickly perceived my state, and taking advantage of it, speedily pulled up my silk robe and elegant underclothing, and muttered, 'Such whiteness and delicacy I never saw in my life before." He proceeded to kiss, mumble, and even to insinuate his tongue into my little virgin treasure. This I know now effected a double purpose; it not only excited me, but rendered my cunt moist and open, so that his cock might have less difficulty forcing an entrance.

Very little of this sort of work was needed before I lay back with my head on a sofa cushion in a half fainting state. Immediately I felt the youth's head, thighs and hips between mine, his head and belly pressed against mine, and his still hotter prick between the lips of my orifice. As yet I was not hurt, but when he found himself in the right road and began to force his way in, I could not avoid a slight scream. He immediately put an end to my protest, rather cruelly I thought, by placing one of the sofa cushions over my face and muffling my mouth effectively. Then with three tremendous shoves he practically split my poor, gaping cunt and so achieved his purpose. I was no longer a maid! After three more ramming thrusts, I felt a warm thick discharge injected into the very innermost sanctuary of my private parts, and my handsome young ravisher sank languidly down on my body, removed the cushion from my face and covered it with kisses instead. Indeed he should have been grateful; he had all the pleasure and I had all the pain. When he had quite recovered himself he begged my pardon for the slight violence he had been obliged to use, and explained that when a young girl has her virginity taken she could not help in ordinary cases screaming a little. For fear of any one hearing me and coming to see what the matter was, he had been obliged to use coercive measures, lest my reputation should be compromised. He then with his pocket-handkerchief wiped my violated cunt, which indeed was necessary as it was all wet with blood and stuff like saliva. This done I felt more comfortable. Then he said he would go downstairs, giving out that it was my orders that I should be served with some chocolate, some jelly, and a glass of liquor. I expressed my thanks at the prospect of this refreshment, on which he further offered to try and get hold of a bottle of champagne. If he could he said he would smuggle it upstairs and it would do us both good.

"Then he took his departure, after tucking in that long and graceful piston, arranging his breeches and smoothing his hair, and trying to look as if nothing had been taking place. As for me, he recommended that I rest myself during the quarter of an hour he

87

would be absent, and look at the remainder of the pictures contained in his wicked and attractive book. There, my dears, in every possible position that a man and the most voluptuous woman could submit to, were the happy lovers represented, with the lady kneeling down, peeping under her belly at her lover's performance, or striding over him taking the larger share of the work herself. To further excite her favorite, I suppose, in some of the photos she was permitting him to shove his prick into what are not usually considered legitimate orifices, such as her asshole, or her mouth...all very pleasant I dare say, but not very proper. However, in this instance, they served Victor's purpose, namely that of exciting me. So that when he returned bringing with him not only the wine, chocolate and jelly, but also the champagne, I felt not only glad of the refreshment, but also of his company. Being further excited by the wine, and his explanations and remarks about the bedroom that night, I told him I would grant him every indulgence that lay in a girl's power, and that if not, we might find opportunities either in the garden by day time or in my mother's apartments when her ladyship was out.

CHAPTER VII

At this period of Emilie's story I noticed a good deal of agitation among the young ladies of her audience.

For instance, Adele was kneeling with her head between the Abbess' thighs; what she was doing I could not exactly see. Emilie herself was sitting with her legs open, perfectly unconcerned, while Louise was fumbling about her secret parts.

My aunt very sensibly remarked, "I think, Emilie, my love, you had better stop a little, for I perceive that narration of your delightful adventures with the handsome young page and the consequent loss of your maidenhead has produced the usual effect upon the minds and bodies of the young ladies present."

I do not know what effect it was producing upon the minds of the young ladies, but I do know what effect it was producing upon the prick of a certain young gentleman. In spite of all my previous exertions, my cock began to erect his ruby head as if to look about him for some new victim. That, as the reader will recollect I could not find very easily, as I had fucked the Lady Abbess and every girl in the room excepting Adele; but as Agnes was sitting upon my knee I had not far to search for the requisite accommodation. Ah, when a man has youth and health on his side, what a choice of delights he has! How easily his course is made clear for him! And how frequently he can repeat his enjoyments, and with what impunity! But enough moralizing. As I began to make known my lustful intentions, to shift the position of Agnes' naked rump upon my knees, she blushingly whispered in my ears, "Dearest Auguste, I am so sore. I fear that I cannot bear your loving embraces any more today." To which I replied that I would rather fuck her than anybody else, but that my animal passions had got to such a pitch that I must really quench the heat and fever of my monster of a cock in some girl's warm pussy told her also that I had fucked every girl there except Adele, and she I had reason to think was kept by my aunt for her own unnatural purpose. This Agnes declared to be nonsense.

In the meantime my aunt, who had been whispering to Adele, called to us and demanded to know what we two young folks were talking about.

"Indeed," she said, "Auguste, we are all rather jealous of Agnes. You have been monopolizing her for the last half hour. She has been sitting, as I can see, with her bare bottom on your bare lap, and Ste. Claire only knows what you may have been doing to her before all our faces." She said all this very good humoredly, but with a little evident spice of jealously.

I replied that neither she or any of the charming girls around us need be in the least degree jealous, for however good my will might be, my sweet friend (upon which Agnes kissed me) felt very sore, and I had too much consideration for any charming girl to force my throbbing weapon into her tender cunt hole when she was sore and bleeding.

I'm afraid, of course, that this was not exactly true and that if there had been no other girl or woman in the room but Agnes, she would have had to suffer either in front or behind, sore or not sore.

As it was, my considerate speech was very well received. Adele especially was very loud in her commendations, and thought I was quite right; no young girl ought to be fucked more than once, at least not on the first day at any rate.

The sly girl knew that I had passed the night with the Lady Superior, that I had fucked Emilie in the morning and subsequently had taken the maidenheads of Louise and Agnes.

So not unnaturally she thought and hoped that perhaps her turn was coming. And I have no doubt but that she expressed herself to this effect in the whispered exchange which I have alluded to as taking place between her and my aunt.

My aunt raised herself from the sofa, saying: "My love, do not distress yourself, you shall have it! I want you to dildo me, for you have had some little experience, more than any of the other young ladies. And dear Auguste shall fuck you at the same time. I know how to arrange it so that his drilling into you while you have the instrument in me will give you additional impetus so that I shall have the benefit of your enjoyment at second hand."

"Oh, that will be delightful," exclaimed Adele, running to fetch the necessary instrument.

Meanwhile my aunt proceeded deliberately to strip off her robe and petticoats, leaving herself in her shift and stockings.

Then she cooly proceeded to examine her luscious, moss-bedewed cunt, pulling the lips slightly asunder and inserting her finger. She worked it in and out, thrusting it inside to the knuckle, then withdrawing it until she merely tickled the nub of flesh that bulged at the threshold of her slit. I hope she found everything satisfactory. Of one thing I am quite certain, namely that I had not hurt her, whatever I had done to the rest of the young ladies. As for me, I was preparing for action by taking off my silk frock and the skirts and flounces which I knew would be in the way of my intended operations. In this Agnes kindly assisted my awkwardness so that when Adele returned to the room stark naked with the dildo strapped around her waist, my aunt was ready to receive her and I to fuck her.

"Ah, you did right to strip yourself," murmured my aunt. "Your stockings contrast very well with her creamy skin, don't they Auguste? And I hope you have got the dildo strapped so as not to interfere with his getting into you from behind. Stoop down with your thighs a little open so that the handsome imposter there can see for himself if he considers the passage clear. In the meantime, I will get myself into the most suitable position—you'll take care of me, and my nephew, with the long legs and standing prick, will take good care of you, I'm sure." Taking this hint I knelt down, pulling open her buttocks, to get a clear view of my path to her tight little crevice.

The dildo was strapped well on her belly, the road to her cunt was free, and I reached under and pulled the lips open. They were smooth and moist, the inner folds had the hue of conch, all pink and shiny. My aunt, in the meantime, had with the assistance of Emilie laid herself down on the table so that her rump touched the edge. When Adele approached her, she threw her legs over the young girl's shoulders, and Adele immediately thrust her hips forward and shoved the ivory velvet-headed tube into its destined receptacle. I, on my part, first slightly lubricated with my tongue the sanctuary I was going to violate, licking all around and within the smiling lips and then introduced my fiery cock-head. I found that the position Adele was occupying relative to my aunt, was an admirable one for my penetrating the very innermost parts of the fine fat-rumped novice.

Moreover, if I had desired additional pleasure I had further gratification in admiring my aunt's finely curved legs and ripe bosom, to say nothing of the sensual gratification expressed on her face as Adele began to warm into her work, assisted no doubt by the vigorous shoves and plunges with which I was penetrating her person. I should mention here, that when I made my third drive into her widely stretched pussy, which was a vigorous one, she gave a slight scream; the only sympathy which that elicited from the others was, "Open your thighs wide, my sweet friend!" from my aunt, "Don't mind her screaming, Auguste! She has got no maidenhead. I took that. Fuck her hard; the road's clear enough!" So I began to ram her brutally while reaching around and crushing her swaying tits with my grasping hands.

Just as Lady Agatha had got worked up to her utmost ecstasy, and required the two or three last heavy thrusts and the injection of the warm cream from the dildo Mademoiselle Adele found herself in exactly the same predicament! This I perceived by her beginning to catch her breath, to wriggle her bottom about violently, to call upon my name with every term of endearment, and to seem to be entirely forgetful of her Superior's open cunt before her. All this was because she felt the rapturous effects of my glorious prick behind her, pounding into her love cave with dogged regularity. All this time my aunt was exclaiming, "Push harder, Adele, harder, you silly girl, and give me milk." But it was too late. I felt Adele losing her rhythm almost helplessly, and it was well for her that I, though on the very verge of spurting into her, still retained my presence of mind.

93

Already I felt her warm lovestream spouting forth and deluging my cock up to the very roots, literally saturating the hair. I saw there was no time to be lost. I caught her firmly in my arms and gave two or three tremendous shoves so as to force the dildo into my aunt's belly as far as it would go. Then, applying my hands to the elastic balls of the instrument, I effected the required ejection to my aunt's great delight. She murmured, "That's very nice. I feared I was going to miss it!" and sank down upon her pillow in a dreamy state of enjoyment.

As for me, I held my fair friend firmly in my arms, and in one second I felt my cock expand to bursting and supplied her with such a liberal allowance of what I may call "essential oil" that it actually overflowed her generous cunt and trickled down her white thighs, showing very conspicuously against her scarlet stockings, to the intense delight of the three girls, Emilie, Agnes, and Louise, who had been by no means unconcerned or even idle spectators of this little drama.

At the very start of the proceedings, I had heard Emilie say to Louise, "Go, dear and fetch me a candle, a good large one. Never mind whether it is lighted at a shrine or not, bring it here." And away ran Louise.

On her return she found Emilie upon the sofa lately occupied by my aunt, her petticoats drawn up, one long leg stuck over the back of the sofa, while the foot of the other rested upon the floor. Of course the exposure of the person was as complete as anyone could desire. Her pink little pussy slit below the generously thatched mount was full open to my hungry gaze and so occupied any glances that I could spare from my immediate business.

On Louise's making her appearance with the candle, a huge one, Emilie told her to insert it in her gaping orifice, a hint which Louise, perhaps inspired by the scene she saw enacted on the table, or a grateful remembrance of my services to her, was not slow to take. She shoved the candle well into Emilie, at least as far as she considered safe. Then she commenced to work it with the judgment of an expert practitioner. And what was poor Agnes doing all this time?"

I rather think that very charming and virtuous young lady was regretting that she had ever pleaded soreness as an excuse for not being fucked. The devotion she was exhibiting toward my person led me to suppose that she would not have been very sorry to have been in Adele's place, sore cunt and all.

For she knelt down, and not only kissed my naked thrusting buttocks repeatedly, but extended her attentions to my cock. She kissed and licked it in such a way as would have raised an erection in the most useless man that ever lived. She slid her tongue along the shaft and balls and even swallowed the head upon its withdrawal from Adele's greedy cunt. Once I'd reinserted it, Agnes returned to whatever of the shaft was exposed to her swirling tongue. Of course Adele had the benefit of the proceedings, though at the conclusion of the act Agnes enjoyed a slight sprinkling of warm cream upon her pretty face.

At any rate, she was the only person among us with any presence of mind or energy to do anything. I sank down in an easy chair, Lady Agatha remained on the table, Adele laid down on an ottoman and Emilie and Louise lay together on the sofa with their arms around each other and their lips pressed together. The candle still protruded from between Emilie's thighs while the melting wax mingled with her own juices. It was an interesting group certainly; a painter or sculptor might have searched the world over for an exhibition of more splendid limbs, or more graceful shapes. A libertine would have been driven frantic at the display of white rumps, mossy cunts, fat thighs, plump bosoms and blushing nipples, all displayed without pretence of concealment.

The effect of this display was heightened by the air of voluptuous languor and total abandonment exhibited by all of us. The only exception was Agnes. She evidently thought that something should be done to preserve a semblance of decency. She first of all turned her attention to me, and I gratefully acknowledged her kindness in wiping my prick carefully and gently with her handkerchief. Then she slipped my frock over my head and fastened it loosely. So I was pretty comfortable, especially after I had gone to the buffet and helped myself to a tumbler of champagne.

Agnes then went and pulled Louise off of Emilie and requested her to put a wrapper or loose frock of some kind upon Adele, at the same time removing the candle and drawing down Emilie's petticoats, so that she was pretty decent. Then she turned her attention towards her Lady Superior, who being pretty well accustomed to such attacks, was not in a very deplorable state of dress. But she gratefully acknowledged Agnes' kindness in drying her cunt and bringing her a glass of wine. Mu aunt proceeded with her help to robe herself, and managed to my surprise and admiration to appear in a few minutes as if nothing had happened.

When order had been thus partially restored, the Lady Superior remarked, "I hope, Emilie, you do not feel too fatigued to continue your story. Ah, you naughty girl," she continued half laughing, "the candle again. I suppose you'll frig yourself to death if you don't take care."

"I beg your pardon Madame," replied Emilie in a languid tone, "On this occasion Louise did my business for me, and very nicely she did it too. When she has a little recovered from her violation I'll do as much for her."

"All very fine," responded Lady Agatha, "but in the meantime as Louise got the candle, which I see is one of the largest and best in the nunnery—and it is a mercy it was not broken by your wrigglings and heavings—she had better go and put it where she took it from, and light it again, and you can go on with your story."

But, just as Emilie was about to recommence, the door opened and there entered Father Eustace and Madame d'Ermonville, or rather I may as well say my father and mother.

Thanks to Agnes' presence of mind, the room and its occupants were better fitted to receive visitors than they had been ten minutes before, but still there was a certain air of disarrangement about the room and furniture. Most decidedly there was something dishevelled in the appearance of the young ladies. Their dresses, though somewhat arranged, were hardly tidy. Agnes and Louise had flushed cheeks and sparkling eyes for their desire had not been gratified, while Adele and Emilie were pale and their eyes heavy. An air of unmistakable sensuality pervaded all four of them. As for me I tried to look as unconcerned as possible, sitting with one arm around Agnes' waist, with her head resting on my shoulder. I suppose we presented a picture of two affectionate young ladies.

Father Eustace seemed determined to carry out the farce and approached me, laying his hand upon my head. "I rejoice, my daughter, that you have made choice of one so holy and virtuous as Sister Agnes for your companion! May your friendship be a close and a lasting one."

I assured him most conscientiously that I intended it should indeed be a close and intimate one, giving Agnes a squeeze around the waist that she understood very well.

Meantime Madame d'Ermonville, after saluting her sister, remarked that she had been taking a walk around the garden with Father Eustace, and was beginning to feel hungry and tired so they had come into lunch. "But I see," said she, "that we are too late as the lunch has been removed from the table to the sideboard."

The Abbess was going to remark that the lunch had never been on the table, when she fortunately checked herself on my mother's remarking, "But you should take care, Agatha, not to let careless people spill melted butter on your handsome table cover. Look here!" And she pointed to the very spot on the edge of the table where her sister's rump had rested, and which had been plentifully bedewed, and which had been neglected in the general robing and cleaning up. My aunt took the allusion very cooly; saying that it was careless, but that she thought it was milk. She requested Adele to wipe it up and invited her sister and Father Eustace to take some refreshment. This they gladly accepted, the holy Father in particular eating and drinking as if he meant to restore his wasted energies.

As they were eating, Madame asked her sister how they had been amusing themselves, and how I had behaved myself. To this the Lady Superior replied that I had conducted myself admirably, (she laid great stress on this word) and had inspired her and all the young ladies with the highest opinion of me. As for their amusements, Emilie had been telling them a short story, relating some adventures of hers, which though doubtless of the world and worldly, and even rather licentious, had doubtless a good moral, as they had spurred her to seek the shadow of the cloister.

This story she proposed to continue as soon as their honored guests had concluded their lunch. On Emilie's expressing her opinion that such a foolish little narrative was hardly fit to entertain such guests as Madame d'Ermonville and Father Eustace, the latter promptly replied that he liked to hear all sorts of stories good or bad, pure or impure. In fact, he rather preferred the latter, as it gave him the opportunity of imposing a suitable penance if he deemed it necessary. Here he glanced at Emilie, who laughed and blushed. "For you must understand, fair daughter," said the handsome monk, turning to me, "that we of the priesthood can do—without sin—whatever we like, provided that our intentions are good."

To this I replied that I had no doubt of it. My mother, turning to my aunt, said, laughing, "I wonder if his intentions were good in the garden just now?"

"Tell us all about it, Henriette," said Lady Agatha.

"Well, I am almost ashamed," said Madame, "but it was thus: I was taking a solitary walk in the garden this morning when I was joined by his Reverence, who after a few commonplace remarks proposed to me that as I had not confessed to him lately, the arbor on the south side of the garden would make a very suitable confessional. I partly guessed what this meant, and, as I expected, very soon found that the first duty of the Confessor appeared to be to shove his hand up the penitent's underclothing, and that of the penitent to stretch her legs open. As I am talking to experienced young ladies, I need not hesitate to say that I received absolution while lying on my back with my thighs wide open, in the shape of a most vigorous fucking, and was favored moreover with a most copious administration of what I suppose was holy oil. Indeed my belly was half full before I sat down to lunch. Well I did not much mind that, indeed I rather liked it."

"Indeed you did," interrupted Father Eustace emphatically.

"But as we were subsequently strolling about the garden picking and eating some of the choice fruits, we met a nun, evidently a handsome woman, but pale faced, whom my companion accosted as Sister Helen, asking her if she had gotten quite well since her confinement..."

"No doubt it was Helen," replied my aunt, "She got in the family way, by some means or other; nobody but herself knows or cares. The child was stillborn and she quickly got well, and I suppose is ready to be fucked again."

"Really!" exclaimed my mother, "listen to me! After a little agreeable conversation, which I joined for I found sister Helen was a most ladylike person, dear Eustace asked her if she had been purified since her confinement. In some surprise, she answered 'no' whereupon he said that it was absolutely necessary that she should undergo that rite immediately, as she was not fit for Christian society in her present state. On this she looked at me with great alarm as if she had been polluting me with her company, and she forthwith consented.

"We were then near the willow tree which stands on the lawn surrounded by laurels. Father Eustace requested his victim to walk with him under the branches of the tree. I followed to see what would happen; we were partially, but only partially shrouded by its branches.

"Then he desired her to stand with her back against the stem of the tree, and told her to take her petticoats and chemise up to her waist, which she did without speaking. Then his Reverence knelt down and forcing her thighs apart commenced to lick her muff with his darting tongue. The curly hair was thin upon her mount, and he wetted it thoroughly until it was plastered to her quivering cunt. Then he proceeded to insert his finger into her pussy and pronounce what he called a blessing and absolution. All I could hear of it was a muttering of 'very tight indeed, quite a maidenhead, four months since she was fucked,' and blessings of that sort. With each word he thrust his finger violently into her envelope, rotating it so that it shone wet and slippery when he withdrew it.

100

"However, proceedings very soon came to an end, for I suppose that Father could not endure his lascivious sensations any longer. Indeed I saw his monstrous prick—you know what a huge tool he carries, don't you Mademoiselle Emilie?—almost bursting through his robe. It appeared that to complete the act of the so-called purification, Sister Helen was to be fucked standing upright with her back against a tree. Pretty purification, thought I, and what's more the gentleman had given me such unmistakable evidence of his power not twenty minutes before, that I should not have supposed him capable of doing another fine woman justice in such a short space of time.

"But obviously there is nothing like change and variety. I am plump and fair-haired, indeed the hair on my cunt is reddish. Now Sister Helen is slender and dark, and the hair of her cunt is black. Moreover, as to minor differences, I always wear white silk hosiery whereas the handsome nun wears black silk. This is very becoming, as I dare say. Mademoiselle Agnes seems very fond of my daughter right well knows, and a very nice display she makes." This remark was occasioned by Agnes having in the fullness of her love passion forgotten herself a little, and crossed her left leg over my right, thus bringing herself a little upon my knee and making a display of her elegant long leg. Agnes blushed, the rest laughed, and my mother went on: "But be that as it may, Father Eustace was quite ready to do full justice to his fresh paramour. Certainly as soon as he could get fairly into her, which he seemed to have a little difficulty at first in accomplishing, though her cunt is not nearly tight and virginal. Finally he gave one upward shove which fairly lifted her off of her legs. I must say that she seemed to reciprocate his ardor, but her position was not the best calculated for displaying her responsive thrusts. Nevertheless she did her best and just as he was getting into the last few powerful digs

101

she lifted up her left leg for him to catch hold of, which he did, thus affording me a fair display. Not only me, as it turned out, but also one of the gardeners who happened to be passing, and who merely giving a glance at the interesting performance said, 'Your blessing, pray holy Father.'

'Benedicite, my son,' replied Father Eustace, drawing out about three inches of his tool as he spoke, and then drove into her and finished her with a deep thrust. And finished himself too, I should think, for he seemed tolerably subdued as he kissed Helen and gave her his blessing. How long he'll remain in his present quiet condition I can't pretend to guess...not long, I'm afraid, if he has any pretty girls to confess especially after such a good lunch and lots of champagne. And now, young ladies, perhaps Mademoiselle Emilie will excuse this interruption, and go on with her story, unless you feel too tired, for I am far too experienced a lady to suppose that any of you have passed the morning in mere conversation. I strongly suspect that there has been a little fucking going on."

"Why, my dear Mademoiselle d'Ermonville," exclaimed Emilie, who was the most forward and experienced of the girls, "who is here to fuck any of us?"

"Ah you know very well, you saucy girl," replied my mother nodding her head and laughing. "Besides, you, if all accounts are true, can manage on occasion without a man's cock—a good sized candle, or even the fingers of one of your pretty companions will give you satisfaction when nothing better is to be had."

This was hitting the right nail on the head and we all laughed so that Emilie vowed vengeance against us and declared that she would tell Madame and Father Eustace all that we had been doing just before they had entered the room.

"Tell away, my child and welcome," said my aunt,

who did not care one farthing who knew, or who saw, for that matter.

Emilie then, without hesitation, proceeded to describe the whole scene that had passed, lingering chiefly on her Lady Superior, Adele, and me, but not omitting herself, and slightly exaggerating the parts played by Agnes and Louise.

"Ah! how I wish I had been present!" exclaimed Madame d'Ermonville. "It seems to me that the most interesting part of the performance was that between Adele and Auguste here."

"My son," said Father Eustace very gravely, "what sort of a rump has that fine girl got?"

I, of course, was lavish in my praise, whereupon he whispered to me, "I suppose you have made Agnes sore; if so, recollect that she has two holes, and if you feel disposed to follow my example with regard to Adele, Agnes will be only too glad to let you do anything."

I did not quite understand him, but held myself in readiness, for I certainly began to feel rather prick-stiffereous.

"Come hither, fair daughter," said Father Eustace to Adele, "and exhibit your posteriors to me; you have never suffered penance from me, I think."

"Never, your Reverence," said Adele, trembling.

"Don't be frightened," said the monk, but bend your head down, and open your buttocks. Have you any pomade, or Florence oil, Sister Agatha?"

"There is plenty of Florence oil on the sideboard; hand it to the Father, Louise," replied my aunt.

"You will never manage it, Eustace," said my mother, who came forward to inspect the priest lubricating the novice's endhole with oil. "She is not very small, certainly, but you are so large."

"I'll manage it, never fear," he said. "Dearest Madame, take Agnes into your arms and hold her there while Auguste performs the same operation on her which I shall do upon Adele. He has taken her maidenhead, and she is sore."

"Certainly," replied my mother, very promptly. "Come to my arms, sweet friend," she said, as she seated herself on the sofa and drew Agnes over her.

"Oh, dear Madame," she exclaimed, "I would do anything to please your handsome, dear son."

"Bring the oil, my Auguste," said my mother, "and oil your prick well, as well as her orifice, and I dare say you'll slip in easily enough."

I lifted Agnes' clothes to her shoulders, and opening her white buttocks, inserted my fingers saturated with oil in the hole I was about to invade. It looked so small that I was at first afraid that I never should manage it; but with a little rubbing backwards and forwards, and gently pulling open, I saw the thing was quite feasible. I was proceeding to oil my standing prick, when a loud exclamation of "Oh!" made me turn around, and I found that what my mother had said was pretty correct—Father Eustace was too large for his intended victim. He could not force his cock-head into Adele's arsehole. "Lay your head on the sofa cushion, dear Agnes" said Madame. "I will prevent that girl being hurt, at any sacrifice. So saying, she rose and said, "Dear Eustace, you really must not; you must not indeed. I would rather you did anything than that."

"Anything, Henriette?" asked the Father meaningfully.

"Yes, anything," she replied, blushing, "though I had rather it not be before these girls."

"Well, I can't wait," replied Eustace, "and you are large enough, that's one comfort."

So saying, he dragged up Madame d'Ermonville's robes in the rudest manner, forced her head down upon the sofa cushions where I had already placed Agnes, and shoved his huge cock without preamble into her small rumphole, or at least it seemed small in

104

comparison with the huge white buttock mounds between which it lay. I followed his lead and pushed the head of my cock inside the starfish-shaped aperture. I experienced great tightness, but also great elasticity, and no difficulty. I could feel every inch of my shaft travel up her anal canal. I am sure that Agnes felt no pain, and if she did not feel pleasure she pretended to do so. My enjoyment was very great indeed, quite ecstatic, and I presume Father Eustace felt equal delight. We thrust in and out with force and speed, our hands on the ample hips of our partners, 'til both of us deluged our fair partners simultaneously with our warm fluid, and withdrew with a noise like the pulling a couple of corks.

Then kissing warmly the rounded snowy mountains we had just been pressing, we arranged our partner's attire, Father Eustace remarking that now Emilie was at liberty to continue her story.

CHAPTER VIII

"Well, Holy Father," said Emilie, addressing the monk, "I am perfectly ready to proceed, that is if you are quite sure that you are done with Madame d'Ermonville and the other ladies. One thing I must say, that the company need not expect to hear anything from me so lascivious as what they have just seen in the performance of you and Monsieur Augustine and your lovely victims, for so I must take the liberty of calling them, considering that their persons have been outrageously violated."

"Don't trouble yourself about us, Mademoiselle Emilie," exclaimed my mother, "Agnes and I are none the worse for what we have undergone. Remember that a rumphole will recover its tightness and elasticity, whereas a maidenhead once burst through is lost forever. And now, please continue your narrative, which I have no doubt will prove exciting enough."

"I think," said Emilie, "I left off where I expected the arrival of my mother. I parted with my seducer and promised him admittance to my bedchamber that night or any night that he pleased. I permitted my maid to arrange my hair and partially to undress me, then I dismissed her, informing her that I proposed to stay up and read for a short time. She obeyed, glad enough to go to bed; and then by way of reading I took from my pocket the small book which Victor had given me, and which I eagerly consulted. Most of the prints I had seen before he violated me, when I was confused and eager. Now I looked at them leisurely, and deliberately; and certainly I must say that every posture which the wantonness of woman or the lust of man could possibly suggest was there delineated.

"Looking at these beautiful pictures naturally suggested to my mind what position my handsome young page would choose to place me in when he came to pay me a visit. This question suggested the idea of whether I was fit to receive him. Willing, I most undoubtedly was, for I began, notwithstanding the ruthless bursting of my maidenhead, to feel very excited. But the wort of it was that my cunt, like those of our pretty young friends Louise and Agnes, was most undoubtedly sore. I knew now what to do; for I felt sure that if my gallant young page could manage by any means to invade my sleeping chamber, he would have no mercy upon me. I recalled that I had some lip salve; this I copiously applied to very different lips than those for which it was intended. Then wrapping myself up in my quilted dressing gown, I determined to wait one hour and no longer.

"Before the expiration of that time the house was perfectly quiet, and I had hardly ascertained that fact to my satisfaction when the room door was opened and Victor entered. His face was a little flushed, but he looked as handsome as ever. I fancied he might have been drinking some wine, but I was mistaken. He flung himself down on his knees before me, and clasped me to his bosom devoured my lips with passionate kisses. As he did so he thrust his hand between

107

my thighs and began to shove his forefinger up my orifice. This I begged him not to do, telling him that I was quite ready to yield my charms to him in any way he liked best, but that having his cock rammed into me would be severe enough without having my little treasure irritated by his finger. I then told him what I had done about the lip salve and he told me that I had acted very prudently, for he could hardly contain himself.

"'Indeed,' Victor said, laughing, 'your passions are very easily raised. Let us see.' So saying, I put my hand to the waistband of his velvet breeches and he, divining my intention, let slip the buttons. Down came the breeches, and lo, there stood his beautiful prick as stiff and eager as if he had not been between a girl's thighs for a month. The veins bulged out in high relief against the fair skin. The head was a dark plum on the end of the shaft. And at the base the luscious grape-like balls dangled below the thick matte of hair.

"He then explained to me that he had been in that heated state for the last ten minutes, and I told him that I supposed that he had been feeling the charms of some of the waiting maids on the stairs or in the corridor, and being interrupted by the approach of somebody had been obliged to run off with his lust unappeased. This I said in jest, for I could pretty well guess that when a page has raised his eyes to his mistress and been so successful at raising her petticoats, he will not chase at lower game, at least not for a while. Consequently I was not much surprised by my young gentleman giving my suggestion a most emphatic denial; but I must confess I was a little surprised to hear him declare that it was no other than Madame La Marquise herself, on her return from the masquerade, that had thus excited his sensual passions.

"'What!' exclaimed I, 'my mother.'

"'Even so, Mademoiselle,' replied Victor, in no way abashed. 'You know the splendid costume in which she was attired, that of a page of the reign of Henry IV. Well, that costume is all very well as long as the cloak and doublet are worn, but when they are taken off, the costume of the lady became more enticing and delicate.'

"He then proceeded to explain that my mother immediately on reaching her own room had complained of the heat, and in the presence of her favorite waiting maid and himself had divested herself of her outward clothing, and exhibited herself in a pair of long silk stockings, 'Considering, Mademoiselle,' he continued, 'that she had very little else on but a velvet cap with a drooping white feather, it is no wonder that my manly passions were excited by her voluptuous form.'

"To this I replied in mock anger that if my mother's more matured charms—the beauty of which I fully acknowledged—had excited his lust, he had better go into her room and tell her so, and see what sort of an answer he would receive. To this he made no direct reply, but begged me to take my delicate hand off his prick, or he might make a mistake and waste his precious juice upon my silk dressing gown. I immediately desisted, and he reflected a moment on the position in which he could fuck me with the most ease and comfort to me, and I presume, to himself. Finally he decided upon what he called the 'flying position,' and upon my asking him what was the peculiarity of that position, he turned over the leaves of the precious volume and showed me a picture of a Turk and a beautiful Greek. The lovely slave was represented as lying at the edge of the bed, on her belly, while her lustful master was holding her by the thighs, one on each arm, so that as he shoved his prick into her, the weight of her rump and body generally forced her down upon him and him into her. This he proposed to do to me, and lost no time in stripping me of my robe. Congratulating himself upon my being such a light weight, he placed me in the required position."

I must here remark that at this period of Emilie's story, I was so much enchanted by the description of this fashion of fucking, that I mentally determined to try the effect upon Louise, who was as light as air itself. Or perhaps Agnes, or both. Emilie proceeded.

"When he had got the lower part of my person rump uppermost, on the edge of the bed, and my thighs resting on the hollow of each of his arms, he steered his cock to my entrance. He rested the burning head on my slit and slowly pushed until the red knob disappeared within. Then he thrust vigorously, drawing almost all the way out before ramming it inside once again. Such was the size, heat, and stiffness of his weapon, that notwithstanding my prudent application of lip salve I could not help a low cry or two. What I would have done without the lip salve I don't know. I wonder if ever a young fellow with his cock well into a girl's paid any attention to her "Ohs and Ahs." At any rate my handsome lover did not; but there was one good thing about him, which was that thanks to his lust and the display of my charms, he expended his fury and sperm shower in about five pushes. My pain, such as it was, was over in a minute. Then covering my bottom with grateful, admiring, and very sensual kisses, he assisted me into bed, and, stripping himself, prepared to follow me. He bolted the door, and proposed to leave the lamp burning, for the purpose he said of seeing when the proper time would arrive for him to leave the room. I also strongly suspect that he wanted to see, as well as feel, the enjoyment of his intended vagaries. As for myself, I felt well inclined for sleep, and when he got into my bed and clasped me in his arms, I laid my hand upon his breast, intending to get some repose if I could.

"After being most generously kissed, I dropped off into a short slumber, but a moment's reflection would have convinced me that short indeed was the slumber that I had any right to expect. For of course, if Master Victor had come to bed only to go to sleep, he might just as well have remained in his own apartment. But at any rate to sleep I went and I recollect dreaming that I was a little girl again, playing in the hay field with my little cousins, and that I was being rolled over in the hay while one of my naughty little friends was feeling what he used to call Cousin Emilie's pretty bottom. I strove to call out that he was rude and that I would tell Mama. Then my dream altered, and I fancied that I had committed some great crime and was to suffer death by impalement, only that the stake was to be thrust through my posteriors and not my belly. My dream was so vivid and real as to this last incident that in striving to cry out for mercy I awoke and found myself lying very nearly on my belly with my face sideways on the pillow. My voluptuous tyrant had oiled both my rump and his prick, and had actually begun his entrance while I was asleep. No wonder I dreamt that my posteriors were being impaled.

"It was no use attempting to stop his proceedings. He had already partially forced an entrance. His knob was in, and I knew it was of no use to ask him to draw it out. I might as well have politely requested a tiger to let go a lamb he had captured. So by way of making the best of the matter I begged him to be very gentle, as I felt that his cock seemed awfully large and stiff for this freshly opened orifice. To do him justice he obeyed me very carefully, and made his shoves very gently and easily until, as I felt, he had got his whole length in, up to the balls.

"And then I presume he had the reward of his gentleness, for he gave three or four rapid pushes, accompanied by the maddest, wildest expressions of delight that I could ever have imagined possible: praises of my loveliness, the beauty of my shape, the grace and length of my legs, the plumpness of my thighs, the whiteness and softness of my cunt—which he was ramming his fingers into—the size of my breasts and the stiffness of my nipples, and finally the peculiar delight and the charms of the hole into which, in the middle of his ecstasies, he had injected a jet of warm thick liquid.

"As he sank down on my body, he burst out into a litany of my kindness, amiability, general loveliness of mind as well as of body. Now all this was no doubt very flattering to my vanity, but of course I had sense enough to know that if I had not been a handsome girl who had surrendered ass and pussy to him I should have heard nothing of my grace of mind or disposition. When my handsome friend had withdrawn his stake and released my tender body from impalement, I told him as much, venturing at the same time a gentle remonstrance upon what I could not but consider an improper and lascivious use that he had made of my person while I was asleep.

"To this he replied that no words were strong enough to express the love and admiration which he felt for me. As for his little proceedings, so far from meaning any disrespect for me by invading the sanctity of my lovely rump, he had meant it as the greatest kindness, for he felt sure that if I had to undergo much more regular fucking I should not have been able to walk.

"'Besides, you know, my sweet Mademoiselle,' he continued, 'that such performances are by no means uncommon, as for instance when a young lady has her monthly courses and is unfitted to receive her lover in the regular way, or when she is afraid of being got with child; or when she is heavy with child and approaching confinement and she is afraid of being injured by a cock being rammed up her cunt. Then, sometimes a lady is impelled by curiosity to feel what the new sensation is like, and a young gentleman sometimes wants a change, or his lust takes this particular direction. Indeed, my sweet mistress, there are a dozen excuses to be made for the rump-hole performance.'

"'So it appears,' said I. "Are there any pictures in that pretty book of yours that illustrate this chaste performance?' This I said as if indifferent, but in fact I very much liked to look at the indelicate pictures, particularly when he explained them in his lascivious way. He at once replied that there were several, and that no book of licentious engravings would be complete without them.

"The book lay on a table beside the lamp by the bedside, so all he had to do was stretch out his hand for it. At the same time he announced that it was half past three o'clock, and that there was no absolute necessity for him to rise before six. But he thought he had better tear himself away from me at five o'clock, so there would be no risk of his being seen, and consequently no suspicion of my character.

"I was pleased to hear him make this announcement, both on account of my own comfort—as I strongly suspected I'd had as much fucking and rumping as was good for me for the next twenty-four hours—and for my good reputation. Having expressed as much, we then proceeded to enlighten our understandings with the pictures.

"You young ladies who understand the subject so well, either from sight of the performance or from actual experience, will probably not be interested in my description of the pictures."

Here she was interrupted by a general chorus of her audience begging her not to omit any part of her story. Father Eustace in particular told her to continue, affirming that her narrative was extremely instructive. At the same time I noticed a lecherous twinkle in his eye, as he glanced at the fair storyteller, which, taken in connection with the nature of the anecdotes she was telling, and his recent disappointment with regard to Adele, seemed to promise that Emilie would not sleep by herself that night, if indeed she slept at all.

She continued: "The first picture shown me was something like the one of the Turk and the Greek I had already seen, only in this one the beautiful woman was forcibly held by a eunuch and a harem attendant in a stooping posture, while her sensual master was effecting a forcible entrance between the snow white cheeks of her rump. This was really a pretty picture but nothing compared to the next he showed as far as brutal lust was concerned. It represented three Indians who had made captive a young Mexican girl and were dividing her amongst them. I don't mean chopping her in three pieces, but dividing the available parts of her person. She was represented as lying on her back on top of one savage so that his prick was thrust up her arsehole; another was kneeling over her face with his tool rammed into her mouth and holding up her legs at the same time, while the third was preparing to fuck her cunt, which was openly displayed.

"The contrast between the hideousness of the brutal savages, and the beauty of their victim, and between their brown skins and monstrous cocks, and her whiteness and delicate parts, was cleverly portrayed; although the picture was hideously licentious, it possessed an indescribable fascination for me.

"I'm afraid that I was beginning to be very sensual, and certainly my male companion did not let my propensities sleep.

"Of course, I did not outwardly show how the pictures and commentary had affected me; but as we lay on account of the warmth of the night and the natural heat of our bodies without bed covering, the effect upon him was remarkably evident—his shirt in the center of his body stuck up in a sharp pinnacle. When

114

I playfully removed the covering, there was his huge cock, stiff as if he had not done any work or play at all. I began gently rubbing it up and down, while I asked Victor what limit he proposed to put to his animal desires. To this he replied that although he had too much consideration for me to propose getting into my body any more for the present either in front or behind, yet there was one way of doing the business which would certainly result in our mutual delight and satisfaction if I would condescend to do exactly as he told me.

"I had got into such a state of mind and body that I was ready to promise anything that would assuage my animal propensities without hurting me. Accordingly, in obedience to Victor's directions, I straddled over his face and presented the lips of my burning cunt right over the lips of his mouth. This posture you will perceive at once, my dear girls, brought my own face down upon his lower parts. Hardly had I got astride upon his face than he pushed his tongue into my open cunt with a delicious tingle as he shoved it in and rolled it about. I grasped his cock in ecstasy when withdrawing his tongue for one moment he exclaimed: 'Into your mouth, my sweet Mistress! into your mouth if you love me!'

"If anyone had suggested to me twelve hours previously the idea of taking a young man's prick into my mouth, I should have scorned the idea as indelicate and impossible.

"But now, with my passions inflamed to the utmost, and with my lover doing precisely the same thing in his way that I was expected to do in my way, I hardly hesitated a moment. I took his magnificent pole into my mouth and commenced sucking it.

"Yes, you girls may laugh, but I assure you in its warm silkiness it was very nice, particularly when combined with the little game he was carrying on between my outspread thighs. He heaved his buttocks up to meet my mouth, and I on my part endeavored with an up and down movement to assist the operation of his tongue. That this gave me more delight than anything else I had yet experienced, I do not hesitate to declare.

"You see his tool was really too large for either of the two holes in the lower part of my body to give me pleasure. Or if it did, it was mingled with great pain. So if his tongue was not too large for my cunt and his cock was not too large for my mouth, where was the harm of our mutually enjoying ourselves in this somewhat extraordinary fashion? Enjoy ourselves at any rate we did. I licked up and down the pulsing shaft, laving the underside from the crown to the balls. Then I swirled my tongue around the bulbous head, which action left him gasping and squirming. But better yet was the moment when I swallowed the entire shaft, feeling the thick piston throbbing in my throat. Just as the ecstatic feeling came over me and I felt that nature could no longer be restrained and that I must let the fountain burst forth—whatever consequences to Master Victor's face and mouth—he also began to heave his rump up in the most furious way while with both hands he pressed my bottom down upon his face. He passed one of his muscular legs over my neck so as to force my face more over him if possible.

"Just then I deluged his mouth and face, but he did not seem to mind it. On the contrary, he continued his sucking and lunging with his tongue, until the same thing happened to me that had already happened to him, and I found my mouth full of a thick warm, salty-tasting liquor. I gulped thirstily until the spasm stopped and I drained him dry.

"Then I got off of him, for I was afraid I was half smothering him, and we lay for half an hour in each other's arms sleepily kissing and hugging.

"Shortly thereafter Victor prudently declared that he must go to his room, as he would certainly fall

116

asleep if he remained longer in my bed, and that it would be better and safer for us both for him to sleep in his own bed. Besides, he said three or four hours sleep would be of great service to him.

"Acquiescing to the truth of this, I let him partially dress himself and depart, feeling sure of the power of my charms to call him to my side whenever I might desire the pleasure of his company. The only thing was to find the opportunity. Reflecting upon this I fell asleep, and did not awake until my maid, Pauline, entered the room about ten o'clock, and desired to know if it was my pleasure to rise. Though usually very respectful, my attendant could not help noticing my pale cheeks, dark-circled eyes and general languid appearance.

"All this I attributed to my monthly courses having come on irregularly, which I also hoped would account for any casual blood stains that might be found on my chemise or bed gown.

"But, as events would show, she was not such a fool as to be taken in this way.

"In the meantime she gave me some chocolate, which revived me, and then I went downstairs to my mother's boudoir to breakfast with her, and to hear her account of the gaieties of the previous night.

"By this time it was eleven o'clock, and I found my mother risen but not dressed.

"She seemed not only tired, but uneasy and vexed, not with me though as I was happy to find out. It seemed that my mother had conceived an affection for Monsieur Le Vicomte de Merville, and as all her efforts (and they were many) failed to bring this gentleman to her feet, she attempted a bold stroke at the masquerade. The Vicomte had often admired a valuable ring belonging to my mother; this it appears my mother had put in a small case and deposited in the right pocket of her breeches.

"When at the Masque she put a small note into Monsieur de Merville's hand, intimating that the crime of picking a pocket might sometimes be forgiven and lead to happiness.

"She was sure that notwithstanding her mask he knew her. 'And you'll hardly believe me, my dear Emilie,' she told me, 'that when the passionless wretch took advantage of my hint and did pick my pockets, though he did it in the grossest way, behind me in the very thick of the crowd and pressing the front part of his person against the back part of mine, and absolutely rammed both hands into the very bottom of my pockets, he never took the trouble to feel my body parts, no, not though the ring in its case lay right against them—the ring he took, of course, but I'll never forgive him, no, never,' exclaimed my mother, half sobbing with vexation to give a man such a fair opportunity, and to have it neglected. 'I expected at least that he would have taken one good searching feel, and requested in my ear a whispered question for something more.'

"'Perhaps, dearest mother, he did not know you,' said I.

"'Then he ought to have found out,' replied my mother with a snuff.

"'Oblige me by requesting Victor to take away these breakfast things, and then you and Fanchette come help me to dress.'

"When Victor entered the room, my mother seemed struck with his appearance. He always looked very handsome, but this morning there was a pallor and a delicacy about his general appearance which was very captivating.

"Perhaps the effects of his rendezvous with his young mistress and his consciousness of it may have had some share in producing these results.

"At any rate my mother looked at him for a minute or two, then said, "Victor, go into my dressing-room and on the floor near the table you will find my garters lying...just bring them here, will you?'

118

Victor obeyed, speedily returning with the small scarlet silk bands in his hands.

"'Now,' said my mother, "kneel down and put them on for me.'

"'Oh, Mama,' I exclaimed, 'can't I do that for you?' You see, I recollected what Victor had told me in the night, and the impression made upon him by my mother's charming person, and I felt rather jealous. I knew that my mother gartered above the knee, and I dreaded the result.

"'Certainly not, child,' replied my mother. 'It is the duty of a page to wait upon his mistress.' So saying as she lay upon the sofa, she deliberately lifted up one leg and drew her silk stocking up to the required height, so that as Victor knelt down to fit on the golden buckled belt, he could not help seeing everything she had to show.

"As he went through the same performance with the other leg, my mother suddenly called out. 'Oh! The wretched flea! Catch it if you can Victor! And you, my child, may leave the room if you like, or stay if you like it better.'

"'Take down your breeches, Victor. The flea is between my thighs and no one can catch a lady's flea in those regions with his breeches buttoned.'

"Victor immediately obeyed, casting as he did so a deprecating look at me, as though to say he could not help it. I need not add that as soon as his stiff prick was set free from the encumbrance of his breeches, all my lady's anxiety about the flea disappeared; she lay with one leg over the back of the sofa on which she was reclining and beckoned him to come on.

"This he was not slow in doing, taking the time however to lay one of the spare sofa cushions under my mother's rump. As he did so I was perfectly astonished at the extent of the charms she displayed; such a glorious pink slit in the midst of such an extensive black forest! And her bottom orifice, which was

119

also displayed by her elevation on the cushion, why it was as large as my cunt! But I had not much time for observation, for the obedient page, always dutiful to his Mistress' commands, reared back and sheathed his weapon up to the hilt in her cunt in two strokes. At the same time he tore open her robe, exposing her fully. Her breasts were ripe and well-formed and tipped with large, rosy nipples. Those mounds jiggled with the force of Victor's persistent thrusts until he grasped them with both hands and crushed them cruelly. I have no doubt he gave my mother perfect satisfaction. Though she kept saying that she did not undergo this operation from any lascivious feelings, but merely as a medicine for her depression, still the broken stammering manner in which she spoke, and the way in which she crammed her fingers into Victor's rump, and put one leg after the other over his back, revealed something very different.

"He pumped her roundly, thrusting in and out, then rotating his hips so as to fully stretch her cunt. He drew back, almost to the point of popping his rod from her, then rammed it into her again and again, almost frantically.

"He finished her at last, then withdrew his sword from its moistened sheath, and commenced buttoning up, while Mama languidly cried, 'Emilie, my child, wipe me dry, and pull down my robes.' I dutifully obeyed but had hardly finished when we heard a carriage drive up to the door. There was a loud ring at the porter's bell.

"'Monsieur de Merville desires the honor of waiting upon my Ladyship,' announced one of the footmen entering the room.

"'Show him into the drawing room, and say that I shall have the pleasure of meeting him there,' said my mother. 'Emilie, my child, summon Fanchette, and accompany me to my bedroom, both of you.'

"No sooner had we arrived in that sanctuary than her ladyship, without assistance, stripped herself completely, while we damped her over with a sponge saturated with perfumed water.

"The next proceeding was a very important one. It was nothing less than washing mother's private parts with a solution of alum. This was to create a fictitious tightness, in the event I suppose, of the gallant Vicomte feeling those interesting parts either with his finger or his still more noble member. And indeed after Victor's performance, something of the sort was absolutely necessary, for both her ladyship's orifices were open, slack and moist.

"After this proceeding we began to dress her ladyship in her most delicate underclothing; then, while Fanchette hastily put her hair into something resembling order, I selected a dark silk morning wrapper, which I considered would become her very well.

"As I was doing so the drawing-room bell rang, and I heard the Vicomte ask the footman who appeared if Madame de Fleury had received his message.

"On my reporting this my mother exclaimed: 'Go to him, my dear child, and keep him quiet and say that I am coming instantly.'

"So I hastened away, and in the drawing-room found a fine, tall gentleman superbly attired, who addressed me as Mademoiselle de Fleury, introduced himself as the Vicomte de Merville, and begged to know if charming Mama would honor him with her presence. I assured him that my Lady Mother would see him immediately, on which he politely remarked that the delay seemed less irksome now that he had a fair companion. Then he made complimentary allusion to my great beauty and likeness to my mother. Then he asked for the honor of saluting my maiden cheek. At this I blushed, and curtsied and tendered my cheek in courtly fashion as I had been instructed. But the cheek did not suit him; he proceeded to the lips, and after fairly devouring them and rolling his tongue around my mouth, he commenced feeling my person, outside my clothes it is true, but still very effectually.

"'Pray keep all this for my mother,' I managed to say.

"'Don't be alarmed, my sweet young friend,' he replied. 'I do not intend any violence on your delicate girlish body, but I am really anxious to see what sort of a daughter your beautiful Mama has got.'

"So saying he lifted my frock and underclothing and deliberately inspected my legs, thighs, belly, bottom and private orifices.

"'Ah, ah!' he said, as he thrust his finger into my recently violated cunt, 'I have found out a secret, eh? Not a maid! And so young, too! Never mind, I won't tell Mama; it shall be a secret between us, but we'll talk about it some other day.'

"I was ready to cry with shame and vexation at having been so soon found out, but he kissed me and soothed me, and I felt somewhat reconciled. Just then my quick ear caught my mother's step, and he had just time to withdraw his hand from my thighs, and I to drop and arrange my clothes, and both of us got a little further apart from each other. My mother entered the room, and very stately, graceful and queenly she looked. Monsieur Le Vicomte said so in very warm language!

"Holding out the ring he had taken out of her ladyship's pocket the night before, he said, 'I found this beautiful trinket last night. It was most delightfully situated. Have I your Ladyship's permission to keep it, or must I put it back where I found it?'

"'Pray keep it, dear Henri, as a token of my regard,' said my mother, 'you can't very well put it back where you found it. You see I have no breeches on!'

"'Pardon me, your Ladyship, I do not see anything at all,' he replied laughing. 'At any rate, breeches or no breeches, the delightful neighborhood is there in all its glorious charms.'

"'Ah! dear Henri, you flatter me!' said my mother smiling and sighing.

"As for me, I began to think it was time for me to leave the room."

CHAPTER IX

"If I had witnessed the familiarities between my handsome Mamma and the Vicomte de Merville a week previously, my natural timidity or modesty would have induced me to leave the room. But I had plucked the apple from the tree of knowledge, and although I had been rather overdone by Victor's amatory proceedings of the previous night, and being naturally of a strong constitution, and suddenly of a very lascivious temperament, I resolved to stay in the room and witness this new performance. I wondered if her ladyship would do her share of the business to the gentleman's satisfaction, after the short but very sharp and decisive fucking she had just subjected herself to from Victor. Moreover I was by no means free from the feminine vice or virtue, whichever you please, called curiosity. So although my mother hinted, 'Dearest Henri, a child is in the room!' neither he nor I paid the last attention to the remark. I quietly ensconced myself in a lounging chair, wondering what shape the Vicomte's aristocratic lasciviousness would take. He on his part was kissing my mother and rolling his tongue around her mouth, while at the same time unbuttoning his breeches.

"When he had accomplished this preliminary, and also raised his shirt, I was perfectly surprised at the appearance of his cock. Victor's was the only one I had hitherto seen, and I thought his was beautiful, and all that a girl could desire—it was a light, healthy flesh and blood color. But this young nobleman's was literally milk white, something like a marble column with a ruby head. I, in my innocence, thought such a pure-looking tool was a proof of his Lordship's aristocratic breeding, but I subsequently found that it was in consequence of his washing it, or having it washed for him, with milk of roses. However, there it stood, which was more at any rate than he did, for my mother playfully pushed him backward on the sofa and began to amuse herself by handling and fondling his beautiful prick and balls.

"'Do be quick, my lovely angel,' said the prostrate gentleman, 'If you are going to ride over me triumphantly, lose no time in gathering your robes up and setting your magnificent rump upon me, for I cannot contain myself much longer.'

"On this my mother called out, 'Emilie, my child, since you are in the room, you must assist me. Gather my robes and underlinen well up to my shoulders, and then as I settle my buttocks down upon Henri, guide his murderous weapon into the open pussy prepared to receive it.'

"I obeyed this order with pleasure, and as her ladyship straddled her handsome friend, I arranged her petticoats and chemise so that she was naked below the waist. Then, as she began to rest her weight upon him, I guided the shining satin knob between the black-haired lips, and it immediately disappeared from view, being swallowed up right to

125

the balls. These I felt: They were hot and as hard as horn. Judging from what little I knew from my own experience, I foretold that the gentleman's enjoyment, or at least the first outburst of it, would be over in less than a minute. His hands were free, for he did not need it to press my mother's face to his; she took care of that, and I only wonder she did not smother him with her passionate kisses and caresses. Instead, he employed them as he pleased, feeling the lady's thighs, and the upper part of her cunt, and crammed his fingers into her arse hole. This I did not consider very aristocratic, but a moment's reflection convinced me that when a man or a woman is in an overpowering state of sensual lust, nothing is too strong, nothing is too gross to be either imagined or executed in the way of gratifying it.

"All this that I am taking so long to relate took only a minute or two to execute. The gentleman's convulsive heavings to meet the lady's heavy downward pressure became more ecstatic, and then ceased almost suddenly, simultaneously with a long-drawn gasp of pleasure.

"I, watched the proceedings narrowly, perceiving that my mother had not quite finished. But as Monsieur's stiffness had not altogether evaporated, she managed by a little judicious rise and fall of her lovely rump to produce the desired effect for herself as well as for her lover! And oh! what a mess they made between them on the blue velvet sofa cover. I was quite anxious for them to recover themselves, so that I might wipe away at least some of the slimy deposit, this was shortly afterwards managed pretty well, and while the enamored pair were putting their dresses into something like order, my mother remarked, 'Well, child, you have seen a very pretty exhibition. I hope it will not put improper ideas into your head.'

"'I should think not,' interrupted Monsieur de

Merville, 'for Mademoiselle seems the very height of prudence and modesty.'

"As I listened to this, and recollected that only fifteen minutes before the speaker had shoved his fingers up my cunt and discovered no maidenhead, I gave him more credit for his gallantry and politeness than his truthfulness. Moreover, to tell the truth, I began to feel rather ticklish and excitable, and no wonder. But my mother did not notice any change in my demeanor; she was asking the Vicomte about a bevy of pretty girls, which rumor said he kept about him, both in Paris and in the country at the Chateau de Merville. A regular sort of harem it appeared to be from her remarks. He took her inquiries, which were half jocular, half jealous, very coolly, and informed us that he always liked pretty girls about him. His housekeepers, both in Paris and in the country, had orders to have always about half a dozen handsome girls on hand, doing easy work, and always at his Lordship's beck and call.

"'Pray, Henri,' asked my mother, 'have these young girls when they enter your service, any idea of the peculiar nature of the services required of them?'

"'Well, dearest,' he replied, as he lazily reclined on the sofa sipping a glass of Curacoa, 'I think it is very probable that they may make a shrewd guess at the truth. Whenever my housekeeper, in Paris, for instance has found a girl that she considers handsome and well-made, she is brought to me for approval, dressed in a short skirt and very little else. I find that I have very little difficulty with the working-class Parisian girls who are very clever, naturally, and licentiously disposed. When one of them is brought into my private room, I naturally proceed at once to examine her legs, thighs and private parts. It is my housekeeper's duty, of course, to ascertain that, if not exactly a maid, the girl is clean and pure, and has not been too hard worked. Such a girl as this generally

127

receives my pokings and fingerings with gratified smiles, and tries to display herself to the best advantage.

"If I approve of her I signify as much to my attendant, who takes special care of her. And if the girl appears very fascinating, I sample her on the spot, making her go upon her hands and knees. Or perhaps, if I am lazy, I settle her rump upon my lap, and have her do the greater part of the work herself. If one of the Parisian girls gets with child by me, she is in due time sent off to the Chateau de Merville, where he is delivered, nursed, and taken care of.

"In this way, you perceive, Madame,' continued the Vicomte, turning to my mother, 'I keep up a very fine breed of peasantry upon my estate, to say nothing of those that strictly speaking belong to the soil. For though the peasant girls about my country house are more modest, than the city girls, the honor of being fucked by the Seigneur is considered so great, that if they did not appreciate it themselves, their parents would take care that if sufficiently handsome they should have the honor of my embraces. And I can say what every Seigneur cannot, and that is that I have never had occasion to force a girl in my life. A most amusing incident once occurred.

"Of course, as everybody knows, the Lord of the Chateau has a right to the first night with every bride that is married. But this is a right I did not always care to exercise, for what with charming ladies of my acquaintance, and pretty girls in my service, I have generally as much fucking as I can well manage to do without injuring my constitution. But the incident was this: a young blacksmith, Pierre Rozeay, was about to marry a girl called Ninon Barbotte. My valet had hinted to me that the girl was rather good-looking but I had at that time some very good-looking girls about me, and felt rather lazy besides. So, beyond sending them a few pieces of gold to promote their wedding festivities, I troubled myself no more about the matter. But, lo! when I was sitting by myself in the cool of the evening, half musing, half dreaming, with a flask of Burgundy by my side, one of my attendants announced that the bridegroom and bride desired to have the honor of speaking to me. I ordered them to be ushered in, fancying that they had come to make their acknowledgments for the trifling present I had given them. They entered, and Pierre, who was usually a very bashful youth, explained his purpose in calling upon me very distinctly and plainly. The fact is, he had taken a few glasses of wine, which had given him courage.'

"'He called my attention to his wife, who was a much more handsome girl than I had been led to expect, and looked particularly good in a white skirt, a wreath of roses around her pretty head, and scarlet stockings that displayed her fine muscular legs. Pierre's speech was to the effect that when Jules the woodman, and Antoine the under-gamekeeper were married, Monseigneur was pleased to honor the ceremony by embracing the brides and taking their virginity. Not only so, but the Vicomte was pleased to express his approbation of the satisfaction he had derived from the young women's personal charms by making each a handsome present on which to commence housekeeping. And when the first child was born, my honor compelled me to say that I would be at the cost of providing for it to a reasonable extent. And Pierre respectfully submitted to my consideration whether he and his bride were not equally worthy of my attentions as Jules and Antoine had been on their marriage. He said that as far as money was concerned that I had behaved very liberally, but that both he and his bride would consider it an honor if I would take her virginity and lay the foundation for a fine child, which would in name be Pierre's, but would in fact be mine and would doubtless be provided for accordingly. All this tickled my fancy amazingly, especially when Pierre lead his young wife forward, and demanded to know if I did not think her very pretty. Certainly she looked so, and blushed very becomingly. But her husband was apparently determined to bring matters to a crisis; for as he stood before me, he grasped her clothes, and lifting them all completely up at one sweep, displayed her naked charms in all their glory. The young rogue calculated well and called my attention to the roundness of her thighs, the size and firmness of her breasts, the length of her legs, the whiteness of her mossy orifice, the virgin purity of her slit. Ninon took this exhibition all in good humor, being apparently desirous of not only obtaining the approval of her young husband but of me, her lord and master.'

"That's right, my lord,' he exclaimed, as he saw me beginning to unbutton my breeches, "you never stuck your knife into a nicer young lamb in your life, I am sure. How will you have her?"'

"'To this I replied that my fancy was that the kneeling posture would suit her best, and that if she was still a maid it was the best and easiest way for me to break through her virgin barrier. No sooner said than done. Two or three sofa cushions flung on the carpet were all that was requisite to make a luxurious couch. The young bride, without any hesitation, at once put herself into position, to the great delight of her pleased and gratified husband, and also to my satisfaction. Her fair white rump was a very fine cushion for my belly to butt against, I assure you, and whether she was a maid or not I neither knew or cared. She was certainly very tight, but I managed to get in right up to the balls the very second thrust that I made. She not only made no signs of suffering any pain, but from the way in which she wriggled her great plump, firm arse about, exhibited most decided pleasure and our mutual joy was consummated after a very brief interchange of shoves and heavings. Pierre, who had watched the whole proceeding with proud attention, remarked at the termination that he could not have fucked her better himself, and thought that I had certainly got her with child. I disabused his mind of this idea; for, be it known unto you, ladies both, that the position that I had adopted with the young bride is not a favorable one for inducing a girl to breed; nor indeed, according to my humble experience, in any position in which the lady's posteriors are presented uppermost. You, my dear Mademoiselle,' continued the Vicomte, addressing himself to me, 'know nothing, of course, about these matters, but it is as well that you should be aware of them, lest in some unguarded moment when you yield up your youthful charms to some forward and favored lover, you should find disagreeable consequences nine months later in the shape of a swelled belly.'

"'Hush, Henri' exclaimed my mother, 'Emilie is far too young to think of such things at present. There will be plenty of time when she is two or three years older, and betrothed in marriage.'

"'Oh, certainly,' replied de Merville, with a glance out of the corner of his eye at me. 'Well, to conclude my story, I assured Pierre that whoever was father of their first child, I would be Godfather to it, on which Ninon curtsied. I kissed her, and slipping a few coins into Pierre's hands. I gave them permission to depart, a happy and grateful couple. I could relate a score of such anecdotes,' continued the Vicomte. 'For example, one day I was overtaken with a storm while on a shooting excursion, and sought shelter in a farm house. There were three very handsome specimens of our country girls there. Their mother offered me the choice of the three to amuse myself with while I stayed and refreshed myself! Very hospitable, wasn't she? Of course I did not refuse such a kind offer, and as they were equally handsome, I chose the eldest, and requested her to show me a bed. The girl, gratified by being selected in preference to her younger sisters, immediately led the way up a narrow stair—more like a ladder indeed—that led to the best chamber in the house. As I followed her I ascertained that she had a fine figure, rather coarse and muscular perhaps, though out of hard labor and exercise, but evidently possessed of the power of satiating the most lustful voluptuary that ever suffered from a stiff prick. You may depend upon it I did not go upstairs with my fine farmer's daughter for nothing. From setting her on the edge of the bed, with her heavy legs over my shoulders and my cock pumping its juice into her belly, to laying her flat on her face in the center of the bed and ramming into her rump. I tried every mode on her to my own satisfaction, and I hope and believe to hers also.'

"'The fun was when Marie and I came into the kitchen again. She looked rather self-conscious, but proud, and I totally unconcerned. Her sisters immediately attacked her with their badgerings, such as: "Well, Marie, how did you like it?" "What did his Lordship do to you?" "Are you sore?" "Let us look." and so on.'

"'To which the worthy mother replied that they should be ashamed and leave Marie alone, for the naughty girls were pulling up her petticoats, and examining her inflamed secret orifices...to see if there was any blood, I suppose. She had Marie sit down and rest herself, and take a cup of cider. Then she turned to me and told me she hoped I had enjoyed myself, that her daughters are very fine girls and she was proud of them, but that nothing was too good for her lord.'

"'To this flattering speech I replied that I had been pleased beyond measure, and the powers of her daughter were so extraordinary that she had fairly forced all my vitality out of me, and that I very much doubted if I should be able to raise an honest erection for a week to come. As I said this, I exhibited my aristocratic cock, looking very nice and white certainly, but dispirited and flabby. He seemed ashamed of what he had been doing, and could not hold up his head. At my speech and exhibition, the good dame burst out laughing, saying that she had not been married for five and twenty years for nothing, and that she could soon put life into me. Indeed, said she, "since it is partly my fault that you are reduced to such a state, I must apply the remedy inwardly, and my daughter Susette, shall administer the outward application. Susette take your hand from under your sister's petticoats. Kneel down before Monsieur the Vicomte, and take his prick into your mouth as far as it will go and suck it nicely."'

She withdrew a dusty bottle from a dark closet and filled a large wineglass. What the liquor was I know not. It was very fiery, but not unpleasant.'

"'The effects, however, were most extraordinary, and almost instantaneous. In two minutes I was at the boiling point, and in ten minutes I was in such a state that Susette, proud of what she considered entirely due to her own exertions, withdrew the beautiful red and white weapon from her mouth, and exclaimed, "See, mother dear, what I have done! Have not I managed it well?"'

"'You performed excellently, my sweet Susette,' I interrupted, 'and now it is your duty to take away the delicious stiffness which you have so cleverly created. Suppose you lie down on the table with your legs hanging over the edge."'

"'Certainly, Monseigneur,' replied the obedient girl smiling. She placed herself in the required position.'

"'I know what you require, my lord, and Jeannette and I will assist you as grooms do with a stallion serving a mare. Pull up Susette's petticoats,' continued the

133

old lady, 'and now open the lips of her cunt and put one of her legs over each of his Lordship's shoulders. Now, my lord, gently at first, she's a maid, I really believe." As the good dame said this, she guided my regenerated instrument between the mossy crimson portals of her daughter's maiden treasure. And indeed, strange to say, for a girl of eighteen, it was a maiden cunt.'

"'My first lunge produced the exclamation of "Ah! Monsieur, how terrible large!" "Oh, Mamma, I cannot bear it!" I tried to stop her mouth with kisses, but as I burst through her obstacle I could not restrain her cries. "Oh, Mamma he has broken through something inside me. His long thing in forcing its way up inside!" Then with some gasping and sobbing she was a finished woman. Her mother stood by gravely approving and pronounced that my performance had been very clever and business-like.

"'I have known and seen the thing bungled many times,' she said, 'I have known a man to spunk between the girl's lips and all over her arse, before taking her maidenhead. I've even known a man fool enough to draw his prick out when the girl began to sob and scream; he loses all his gratification, and the young woman does not thank him for the self-denial. She wants to know the secret of the proceeding. She knows other girls like it, and she knows she will have to bear it sooner or later. Depend upon it, my lord, there is nothing like a gentle violence, not that all maidenheads are equally difficult to burst through.'

"'No, indeed," I replied. 'I have taken at least a hundred, but your daughter's was remarkably tough, the strongest resistance I ever met with; I'm afraid she'll be very sore tomorrow.'

"'Never mind, my lord,' said she, 'I will wash her with milk and water, and she shall keep quiet. Bless you, sir, she'll be fit for fucking again in forty-eight hours!'

134

"At this I laughed and said that I should be happy to see either of the fine girls whose embraces I had just revelled in, or their sister Jeanette, whose person I had not enjoyed, any day they chose to pay me a visit at the Chateau.'

"'But I weary you, my dear Madame, and your fair daughter with the history of my rural adventures, and indeed, it is high time for me to take my departure. At what time tomorrow may I have the honor and pleasure of calling?'

"My mother assured him that she would be delighted to see him at any time after noon. He bade us adieu, kissing my mother in a most lover-like manner, and respectfully saluting my hand. I could not help thinking as he did so, however, that there was a wicked gleam in his eye, and that he meant more than he dared show.

"After he had departed, my mother said, 'Emilie, my child, as you perceive, I am no prude, nor do I wish to bring up my daughter as a prude. I certainly should not wish you to have a child before marriage or to compromise yourself grossly in any way. A little loving enjoyment with a young gentleman of good family, or even tasting the joys of passion in the embraces of a married gentleman who is honorable and knows how to hold his tongue—anything of this sort, prudently and moderately enjoyed, I will not object to. But I warn you that I will not have you interfering between me and my lovers! All men like change, I know; some men have a particular penchant for very youthful girls. I myself was ravished by violence in the garden of a summer house when I was young, and before I had anything but a little mossy down on my private parts. My violator was a nobleman who had one of the handsomest wives in Paris and she certainly ought to have satisfied him. But he explained to me as a sort of apology for his dreadful crime, (I'm sure I thought I was fairly split, and that

135

my cunt would never come into shape again) that he had an inexpressible craving for a very young girl, and that he felt he must gratify his longing at any risk or cost. I only tell you this to show that you may not only be sought, but well-fucked too. I warn you that if you admit Henri's beautiful cock between your thighs, or take any of my other particular friends into your arms, I will send you away...to a convent, most likely.'

"Of course I promised my mother most faithfully, and certainly meant to keep my promise. Whether I was able to do so or not, my dear friends," continued Emilie, looking around to us, her circle of attentive listeners, "You will be able to guess, judging from my presence here among you. The crisis of my fate was soon to arrive. On the very next day, about noon, a message arrived for my mother. It said that her aunt, a very rich old lady who lived about six miles from Paris, was dying, and her presence was urgently requested. Now my mother had great expectations from her aged relative, so although she greatly disliking leaving Paris at any time, and particularly after making engagement with Henri de Merville, she most reluctantly but speedily made her arrangements for departure. She wrote a note for Henri, informing him of the necessity for breaking their appointment. She begged him to see her the next day. I, of course, was not supposed to be at home. And away she went. She had not been gone five minutes before I saw the Vicomte's carriage drive up to our entrance, and listening, I could hear Henri expressing disappointment at Madame's absence. But, instead of going away, he announced his intention of stepping upstairs to write a note. To this, of course, the porter could make no objection, as he was well known as a favored guest. So one of the footmen ushered his Lordship upstairs, supplied him with writing materials and wine and left the room. Now I had just left this very room, being under orders to keep out of the way of my Mamma's pet; but finding that the coast was clear, and not hearing anyone about that would be likely to intrude; feminine curiosity, and indeed, perhaps a stronger feeling, induced me to trespass into my mother's sitting room under pretense of looking for a book. Of course I acted quite surprised to find the Vicomte there and prepared to withdraw, feigning great modesty, and regretting my Mamma's unavoidable absence.

"'Oh, I know all about that, you know,' said the Vicomte, very cooly. "I dressed up a servant of mine in your aunt's livery, and sent him here with a fictitious message in order to get your beautiful mother out of the way. Kind and yielding as she is, I know she would half kill us both if she caught us in each other's arms.'

"Well, I knew pretty well what all this meant, so obviously the first thing to do was to lock the door to prevent intrusion, if not listening. Of the latter we would have to take our chances. Any hesitation I might have had about my next proceeding was obviated by the handsome young nobleman catching me on the sofa, where he perched me upon his knee, first of all lifting up my petticoats so that I sat with my posteriors and thighs naked. When he got me thus, he covered my lips with amorous kisses, and then proceeded to say that he knew I was no virgin; and as he said so his inquisitive fingers at once penetrated my secret recesses. He did not care how it had happened, whether I had done it myself or whether I had it done for me, but at any rate he hoped I would not refuse him the pleasure of revelling in my budding charms. Now I had not been fucked for thirty-six hours, and what with witnessing my mother's performances, and listening to her lover's lascivious stories, I had got myself into a considerable state of heat and excitement. So that the only reply I made, and I suppose it was the best that could be made under the circumstances, was to clasp him tenderly around the neck and press my hot lips to his. Upon this he gently laid me down upon the sofa, previously placing a sofa cushion for my soft posteriors to rest upon. Then, separating my thighs, he began first to kiss my cunt, and then to lick it, until I thought he would end by eating it altogether. He abstained, however, from that demonstration of his passion, and apparently unable to wait any longer, dropped his breeches and got upon me, lifting my legs out of his way as best he could.

"He began his work very slowly indeed, but it was very delicious. He was large and strong, but very gentle. On one occasion after giving an extra shove he hoped he had not hurt me, and that I liked it. Didn't I! I raised my legs and crossed them over his back and heaved myself up more vigorously, I thought, than he shoved into me. He thrust hard into the rearmost portions of my cavern, drawing himself out nearly to the head only to plunge fully within once more. He did this more and more quickly until our common notion became frantic and bestial. At last it came, the delicious natural emission, drowning his cock and wetting both him and my bottom. And now I perceived that he had an object of not finishing at the same time that I did, for as I lay half fainting, he whispered, 'Sweetest Emilie, if I had yielded to the dictates of nature at the same time as yourself, the effects to you would probably have been most disastrous. But I have controlled my longing desires in this tender little orifice, by which proceeding you will run no risk of a swelled belly.' As he said this he proceeded to moisten my rumphole with the milky emission that he had sufficiently moistened from the former orifice and enlarged it with his finger. He rolled me over on the sofa and lay over me again, this time, however, on my bottom and not on my belly. I made no objection to his proceedings, feeling it only just that as I had all the pleasure to this point, he should have his share also. Moreover as Master Victor had travelled the road Monseigneur proposed to travel, I did not feel much alarm as to the consequences. He was larger, however, than Victor, but decidedly more gentle, and as he had been restraining himself for the last three minutes, it naturally followed that when he gave the rein to his passions, his proceedings were not very lengthy. He inserted the slippery end of his cock into my endhole and gently eased the shaft within. I felt pleasantly full of his prick and pushed back against him. Of course, I did not count his pushes, but I should think his performance did not last much over a minute. Then he deluged me.

How long he would have lain upon me, enjoying the soft cushion my buttocks afforded him, I know not, but I ventured to remind him that his carriage and horses had stood at the door for half an hour. Writing a note would hardly account for his passing such a long time in the house, and my mother's jealously would most undoubtedly be roused. He acknowledged the truth of my remarks and kissed me passionately, swearing that he would find means to meet me again. Then I slipped out of the room, preparatory to his ringing the bell and ordering the note he had written to be delivered to Madame immediately upon her return.

CHAPTER X

"Immediately upon leaving the Vicomte de Merville in my mother's apartments, I proceeded to my own room wishing to refresh myself with sponging, and also to change my dress. In passing through a narrow corridor which connected my mother's suite of rooms with those appropriated to my own use, I met Victor. Now it must not be supposed that my admiration for my new aristocratic lover had altogether obliterated the regard I felt for Victor. On the contrary, I felt very warmly and passionately toward him as I believe every girl must feel towards the man who has first invaded the sanctity of her virgin precincts.

"There are more experienced ladies here than I am," said Emilie, addressing herself to the Lady Superior and Madame d'Ermonville, "and I will appeal to them whether there is not a certain feeling of affection when a certain amount of force, of course, I do not mean brutality, has been used.

"Both ladies thus appealed to, confirmed Emilie's

opinion, and begged her to continue her interesting story.

"When I met Victor he gave one rapid glance around and covered my cheeks and mouth with amorous kisses. From so doing he was about to proceed to take further liberties; indeed, he had already grasped the front of my dress, but I had no notion of allowing him to get his hand between my thighs just then. In the first place, my passions had just been completely satiated; in the second place, I felt a little sore; and in the third place, both my orifices were wet and slimy, as indeed was also my chemise. And of course, the handsome youth was quite clever enough to figure out what was meant by such signs and tokens, and I had no notion of his making any such discovery. So I whispered to him that I felt sore, and unwell and sickly. As this assertion was corroborated no doubt by my pale and languid appearance, he had the good taste to desist immediately.

"But my sweet Mademoiselle," he began plaintively, "What can I do? Look here!" So saying he pointed to the center of his velvet breeches, into which it seemed as if somebody had stuck a fair-sized cucumber or rolling-pin. Indeed, it seemed greatly to the credit of the tailor that the bottom part of Victor's britches held together at all. I laughed and told him that he ought not to have given way to his lascivious ideas; and that there was no reason at all why a young page's prick should stand up in such a terrible way merely because he met his young mistress in a narrow passage. But as his state of mind and body seemed to be beyond a joke, I suggested to him that there were plenty of young girls in the house—there was Fanchette, my own maid, and Sophie, my mother's chambermaid, either of whom would be happy to receive his embraces. And this I said, not because these girls conducted themselves with impropriety, but because I knew it was the nature of all young

141

Parisian girls in their positions to yield possession of their persons cheerfully to any handsome young fellow who would exhibit a little passionate admiration towards them. This was especially true in the case of a youth like Victor, who was not only extremely elegant in his appearance but was suspected of having a nobleman for his father.

Victor grumbled a little. The suggestive voluptuousness of his honored lady, and the virgin charms of her lovely daughter, had quite soiled his appetite for any common meat, he said. But I stopped his nonsense by assuring him that as far as my attendant Fanchette was concerned, she was as sweet a girl as ever lived, and that her young charms were a banquet fit for any duke or marquis in France; that I had seen her stripped, and that her thighs, posteriors, and belly, and shape generally, were very nearly perfect. Of course, if he did not like her he might let her alone; but that I told him I was going to ring my bell for her to bring me up some warm water, and that if he chose he might go in instead and tell her what I wanted. This I said somewhat indignantly, but he thanked me cordially, and proceeded on his errand.

"'Tell her to take it into the bedroom, Victor,' I said. 'I shan't intrude upon you for ten minutes. And mind you don't thrust your hand up her petticoats as she comes upstairs, or perhaps she will spill the hot water.'

"'I intend to make her spill something better than warm water, my dear Mademoiselle!' said he, laughing, and away he went.

"While he was gone I partially opened the door of communication between my bedroom, and dressing room, and by shooting the bolt, prevented anyone closing it completely, if even they had been so disposed. Then, seating myself in an easy chair so as to command a view through the aperture thus left, I awaited the drawing up of the curtain (meaning

Fanchette's petticoats), and the opening of the play, (the opening of her thighs and cunt). I had not long to wait.

"Enter Fanchette, bearing a large jug and with Victor's arm around her dainty waist. She was half laughing, half indignant. 'Do be quiet, Victor!' she said. 'Really you are quite indelicate. If my young mistress knew, we should both be turned out of the house...at least I should. As for you, you impudent fellow, handsome pages are always appreciated, and perhaps you might retain your place. Do be quiet, you saucy boy!'

"This was said as Victor thrust his hand up the front of her petticoats, feeling her cunt, I presume. At any rate he made a fine exhibition of her legs and thighs.

"His proceedings were making a favorable impression upon her as I could perceive, and when he told her that her mistress was not coming into the room for ten minutes, she turned a languishing look towards him, laid the jug down, and sighed.

"By this time he had her clothes up all around her to her waist, and was on his knees feeling and kissing her rump, thighs, and belly, and the little orifices secreted in the neighborhood thereof. As he did so, with his left hand he was clumsily and fumblingly unbuttoning his breeches. At last this was accomplished, and he rose from his knees. His cock, freed from its confinement, sprang loose, in full erection and ready for work.

"Then grasping my pretty attendant around the waist he half-led her, half-carried her to my bed, where he perched her on the edge, and dragging a pillow out of its place, thrust it under her head. Then taking a leg in each hand, he proceeded to work without further ceremony. But he didn't know his hostess; for Fanchette proved to be, if not quite a maid, at any rate very close and small. Moreover the lips of her cunt lapped over each other more than is usually the case. The result of this was that Master Victor made one or two very earnest shoves without effecting an entrance. If I may make use of the expression, he was doing nothing more than knocking at the door for admission.

"At last, in the agony of his unavailing pushes, he murmured, 'Put your hand to my prick, my sweet little friend, and guide me into the heaven of bliss, or else I shall come all over your belly, and you will have no satisfaction at all, and I very little.'

"Fanchette, who had been giggling at his unavailing attempts, now saw that the matter was becoming serious, and perceived that from having an arm under each of her legs, his hands were not at liberty to help him. So she reached with her delicate little right hand and guided his greedy monster of a prick into her mossy cushion. By way of rewarding her pains, he shoved the entire length of his tool—nearly nine inches, I should think—right into her with the very first thrust, which I thought very reckless and cruel.

"Poor Fanchette screamed out, 'Ah, Victor, have mercy! I cannot bear this dreadful cock tearing up my inside. Ah! Do not, I beg you! Oh dear, dearest Victor! Ah me!' and here, as he sunk gently down upon her bosom, covering her face and white bosom with kisses, she gave vent to a long drawn sigh, and I could see that the page after a few more driving thrusts had managed to effect her pleasure at the same time that he consummated his own.

"You will notice, my kind hearers, ladies and gentlemen all, that my pretty attendant's note altered considerably from the sharp pain she suffered from the first shove, to the deep sigh of gratified sensuality that marked the termination of the youth's labors. And I think it should be so in every case where a girl is judiciously fucked, however tight she may be, or however hugely proportioned her male friend may happen to be. A man who thinks of nothing but shoving his standing cock up a girl's cunt, and spurting into her as soon as he can without any reference to her gratification, is, I think, little better than one of the lower order of animals."

This remark of Emilie's excited universal agreement among the assembled circle. Even dear little Louise, who I am sure had not been particularly well-used by me, murmured her assent to the principal laid down by her more experienced friend. Good Lord! thought I, wondering what a girl or a woman would not put up with from a man once her desires are stimulated. I was sure nothing short of a man's strong embraces or in plain language, a downright good fucking would satisfy her sensual longings.

Then Emilie continued her tale: "By this time I thought I might announce my presence. So getting up from my seat, I went to the outer door, which I opened and shut as if I had just entered my dressing room. This had the desired effect: I could hear Victor get up and beat a hasty retreat. I presume he must have buttoned himself up outside the bedroom door. At any rate when I entered I found Fanchette alone, hastily replacing the pillow and putting the bed into something like order. I told her to get me a clean chemise, and meanwhile I stripped myself and then desired her to sponge my private parts.

"The astonished look on Fanchette's face upon hearing this is hardly describable. She stared at me as if she thought her young mistress was either out of her mind, or more likely, had strangely forgotten herself with the last hour. I only laughed at her, and said, 'Never mind, Fanchette, it is what all pretty girls must submit to sooner or later.' This I said as Fanchette was carefully sponging and drying me.

"Presently she said that she had no right to ask who had the presumption to violate Mademoiselle's person, but she feared that whoever it was had not been satisfied with what was usual in such cases, but had been guilty of double rudeness. From what she said, I suppose she detected that the Vicomte had been amusing himself with my rump as well as my cunt, but I treated the matter with indifference, and requested her to assist me to dress. As she was doing so, I said, 'Don't you think, Fanchette, that a little washing and bathing would do your secret parts good?' My faith, how she colored up! Her face became the color of scarlet in one moment.

"'Why, does Mademoiselle imagine—?' she began.

"When I stopped her by telling her I had just seen her and Victor amusing themselves on the edge of my bed, she with tears begged of me to excuse the liberty she had taken with my bedroom. 'Indeed, Mademoiselle, that saucy young fellow was so loving and looked so very handsome that an indescribable sort of feeling got over me, and I let him do what Mademoiselle saw, so I need not describe it.'

"At this time I heard a carriage drive up, and the porter's bell ring. Rightly conjecturing that my mother had returned, I hastily assured Fanchette of my sympathy and good will, and felt sure that the gratitude which she exhibited and evidently felt would be a safeguard against her tattling or telling tales about my requiring sponging and a clean chemise.

"I met my mother as unconcernedly as I could, but she was in a high state of indignation on finding out that she had been duped. Her aunt was as well as she herself was, and, what was worse, seemed likely to remain so. The note requesting her to visit the old lady was a forgery. My mother, perceived at once that it was a plot to get her out of her own house, either to take advantage of her absence from home in some way, or to rob her on her journey. Finding that robbery was not attempted, she jealously came very near guessing the truth. I could see that her suspicions were aroused by the strict way in which she cross-questioned me about the visit of the Vicomte. I brazenly described that I heard he had called but I had not seen him. In making this assertion I think I went too far, as some of the domestics must have surmised that I was in the salon when he called and, without meaning any harm to me, would have no hesitation in admitting the fact. Whereas, if I had stated that I had seen him for a few minutes, and that he had written a note to be delivered to her Ladyship, no one could have actually proved that we had had any amorous intercourse together. In either case I would be telling a falsehood, but as it happened, the lie I told was almost more than my mother could swallow, and I very soon found out the consequences.

"In the meantime, however, my mother pretended to believe me, and I flattered myself that I had deceived her. I very soon found out that I was mistaken.

That night, I retired to rest hoping that the next day I might have the pleasure of seeing the Vicomte, and if the fates forbade our having any rapturous enjoyment together I might at any rate console myself with Victor. But I was doomed to disappointment in the first instance, and very nearly in the second also. For, when I descended to the salon about midday, having breakfasted in my own apartments, I was informed, to my great surprise that my mother had already dined and hurriedly left the house about an hour or so ago. And this in one of my mother's late habits was very remarkable and set me wondering where on earth she could possibly have gone. It was quite three o'clock before she returned; when she did I was summoned to her presence and I saw at once that her stern aspect boded me no good.

"'Emilie, my daughter,' she began, 'you told me a gross falsehood yesterday; you said that you had never seen the Vicomte de Merville. Now I have seen him today, and he admits having seen you, but only during

147

five minutes brief conversation. But his confused manner, joined to the downright lie you told me, have raised in my mind the very worst suspicions, and in defiance of my warnings to you, I feel quite sure that you have taken my favored lover into your embraces. To speak plainly, you have let him fuck you. I dare say it was more his fault than yours, but that is no safeguard for the future; for when a girl has once tasted the sweets of being well-fucked by a handsome young man, she will not rest satisfied until she has it again.'

"Here I began to stammer out a denial but this was speedily cut short with, 'Take up your frock and under linen if you please, Mademoiselle!' There was nothing for me but to obey, and now I knew that my detection was certain. As I displayed my naked form, my mother muttered, 'Ha, very full-shaped for a young girl! Fine thighs and buttocks indeed, not so magnificent as my own, but very attractive. I doubt not everything very nice and clean, but rather an appearance of irritation, too. Open your thighs!"

"As I did so my lady inserted her forefinger into my cunt as far as it would go, and then nodded her head knowingly, exclaimed, 'Just as I expected, no maidenhead! Thoroughly well-fucked of course, and as Henri does not stick at trifles, the rump hole broken into also most likely. Well, Mademoiselle, I have only just this to say, that feeling perfectly confident of discovering what I have just found out, that on my way back from Monseigneur de Merville's I have called on a friend of mine who has interest with the Superior of the Convent of Ste. Claire, and she has written a letter of introduction which will procure you admittance, not as a nun, but as a guest in retreat as it is called. And there you will have leisure to calm down those sensual desires that a child such as you has no business with. And until you leave my house, I shall keep a watchful eye over you.'

"I was very much grieved to hear this. But more than that, I was annoyed, and being strong in spirit, I determined not to show my feelings. I consented calmly, merely saying that I should like Fanchette to assist me in packing up my clothes and trinkets.

"My mother assented gladly, for she was pleased to see how cheerfully I received her sentence of banishment, adding however, that I would have very little use for my trinkets. These, however, I was determined to take, as valuable property is always useful to carry about with one. Then I left her to seek Fanchette.

"As I passed along on my way to my apartment, by fortunate chance I met Victor. I hurriedly whispered to him to hide himself in the bath adjoining my dressing-room, and that I would join him there presently. He nodded assent with a beaming face, and I passed on feeling that there at least we should be safe from intrusion, that sanctuary being reserved for my exclusive use. If I had made an assignation with him in my bedroom, there would, of course, be Fanchette, not that I minded her presence, but my gracious mother might step in to see how my packing was going.

"Entering the room I rang the bell, and on Fanchette's appearing directed her to set to work at once and to make a considerable selection of some of the best and most valuable of my dresses. The affectionate girl burst into tears when she learned the reason for these preparations. But I had not much time for comforting her, as I knew Victor would be getting impatient, and, what was more, might be missed if someone else wanted him. So I sought the small bath chamber set apart for my convenience, and on opening the door found my handsome page sitting down on the closed seat with his breeches down. He was in a tremendous state of expectation and his cock reared up between his legs like a cobra responding to the summons of the pipes. No words passed between us; I bolted the door, and he rose from the seat. At the same time he gently pressed my head and shoulders forward, so that I was in a stooping position with my buttocks well stuck out. When he had me placed to his liking, he turned my clothes up over my shoulders and immediately began kissing my well-rounded cheeks—the cheeks of my rump, of course. And then he set to work. The position, which I believe is called horse and mare fashion, is a very favorable one as long as the girl has anything to rest her arms upon and the circumstance of my one leg upon the seat must have given him a good view of my juicy cunt, and enabled him to charge in at once without any fumbling or boggling. His thick scarlet head separated my tingling pussy lips. Then the burning shaft followed, inching up my hungry passage. So hard and thick was it that I felt its entire length scraping my inner membranes. Thanks to my dearly bought experience with the Vicomte, and my subsequent rest and washing, I felt no pain, nothing but pleasure. And when the ecstatic moments arrived following the frantic pumping and I felt Victor's noble prick advance an inch further up my insides. He let loose a copious injection of warm fluid. I responded most generously with an equal amount, and we were both very happy and pleased with each other. Of course we could only speak in a whisper, but Victor managed to make me understand and that he would move heaven and earth to get leave to accompany me as one of my attendants on the following day, and that he thought he knew how he could manage it. I was curious to know how, but there was no time for talking. I went to my bedroom leaving my friend to slip away quietly and at his leisure, which I suppose he managed adroitly enough.

"That evening I received an invitation to join my mother for dinner. This was an unusual favor, for she seldom supped at home and when she did her companions were generally merry gentlemen and ladies of the court, whose manners and customs she did not wish me to observe. But this evening, in honor of my departure, I suppose, she was pleased to invite me to a tête-à-tête repast. A very good supper it was, too. The only negative note was an expression of disgust on her part at Victor. That lad, as she called him, sent in a request by the steward, he might be allowed to form part of my escort tomorrow, as one of the footmen. My mother proposed to send with me three armed footmen; with the coachman, she considered this sufficient protection. For my convenience, Fanchette, was to ride with me inside the carriage, then leave me and my boxes in the convent, and return by herself.

"'Bye the way,' said my mother in a musing tone. 'those rascals of footmen will be fucking Fanchette into fits on the journey home, probably knocking her two holes into one, or something of that sort. Of course, it can't be helped, and I dare say she is used to it. But as for that lad, Victor, pretending that a little country air would do him good...it is all nonsense!' Then, ringing the bell, she told the footman in attendance to leave, and send Victor in his place as she wanted to speak to him.

"'So Victor,' she said, on his entering, 'how long have you been ill, and what is the matter with you.'

"'Not ill at all, my gracious Lady,' he replied, 'only weak, languid and sickly.'

"'Weak and languid! Nonsense!' exclaimed Madame. 'Here, sir unlace my boots, and then bring me those embroidered slippers.' So saying. she stuck up one of her dainty feet. Victor, as he stooped down to unlace her boots, could not avoid seeing up her petticoats. I could not help smiling inwardly at this test for proving the truth of the young fellow's assertion of 'weakness and languor.' I fervently hoped that her ladyship would find herself disappointed.

151

Indeed when I recollected the noble way in which Victor had fucked me a few hours previously, I entertained some hope he might manage to dupe her.

"And so it was. Madame elevated first one leg and then another, so that the whole extent of her white silk stockings, and even part of her bare thigh was visible to me, what then must Victor have seen? Notwithstanding this, when his mistress bade him take down his breeches, there was his cock, sleepy, stupid, and limp, hanging down its head.

"'Well, upon my word,' exclaimed my mother. 'the poor dear boy must be unwell! I never exhibited my charms without effect in all my life before, but it is quite evident that you are no use in this house just at present. So, if you think that a little change of air riding behind a carriage for a couple of days will do you good, you have my permission to form one of Mademoiselle's party tomorrow.'

"'Thanks, gracious Madame,' said the page, kneeling and kissing her hand.

"Our journey next morning commenced as arranged by my mother. Fanchette was with me inside one of our carriages which was big enough to hold six people with ease. One armed footman rode on the driving seat with the coachman, and Victor and another, also well armed sat behind us. We were to reach the convent that night. Then the men and horses were to rest at a neighboring village, and return to Paris the next day.

"Part of the road winding through a forest was the reason for our requiring armed men. But, the only incident that occurred during our journey through the forest was this. It seems that Victor's penchant for Fanchette was well known, and he was frequently ribbed about in the house. It was supposed that he had managed to get himself appointed one of my domestics for the sake, if opportunity offered, of fucking Fanchette. This was explained to me afterwards, by Victor.

"While we were going through the forest very slowly, because the road was bad we overtook a peasant girl riding to market on her donkey. As we passed I merely remarked that she was a fine girl with a sunburnt face, and that her baskets caused her to straddle to an alarming, and, I should imagine, uncomfortable extent. This also had the result of exhibiting her muscular red-stockinged legs well up to the knee. However, we passed her, and I thought no more about it. But suddenly the carriage stopped, and Victor came to the window to announce that one of the horses had thrown a shoe, and that we must be detained ten minutes.

"'The fact is Mademoiselle,' Victor whispered, 'that Robert and Phillippe mean to fuck that fine country girl we passed just now. They will take her up against a tree or any other way. They have persuaded old Jacques, the coachman, to pretend a horse has cast a shoe, and I have given them a gold piece each, and a bottle of wine. In exchange they will say nothing about my riding inside for the remainder of the journey.

I laughingly told him that he was a capable manager and that Fanchette and I would be very glad to have him inside. I did not say inside our persons; but I have no doubt from his subsequent proceedings that he understood it so. Moreover, I expressed the wish to see the country girl performed upon, if only to see how it turned out with the two footmen. Accordingly, when she came past the carriage the two of them placed themselves on each side of her. Immediately, Robert began kissing her handsome, healthy face, while Phillippe had his hands between her arse and her cunt. She began to struggled and scream, but I told Victor to give her a crown, and to tell her submit with a good grace. I wanted to see her well-fucked and my time was precious.

"On this she altered her tone considerably, merely saying that two such fine big men, one after another, was too much for a poor girl to bear. Phillippe laughingly replied that this objection could be easily disposed of, and the whole party of us marched to where some bushy trees made a thick screen from the highway.

"Robert and Phillippe began to unbutton their breeches as they walked along. Arriving at their destination, the first thing they did was to take a cord from one of the girl's basket and tie her clothes to her armpits. The whole of her vigorous healthy person was displayed in the most bare-rumped, but not bare-faced, manner. Then pulling her thighs apart so that she stood somewhat astride, Robert plunged his stiff prick into her cunt and Phillippe began to work his way into her rear. They lifted her quite up to her tiptoes, and almost off her legs by their lunging shoves.

"Phillippe said as well as he could between pushes, 'You—see—my rural beauty—that—we—are—rather pressed for time—and as you—seem—to—object—to us—one after another—we have considered your convenience—and our own, too—by fucking you both together. How do you like four balls hanging against your arse, all at the same time, eh? Nice tight rumphole you've got! How are you coming on, Robert?'

"'Oh, I'm up to her kidneys,' was the other footman's reply. "She's spouting so that she's nearly drowned my poor cock—oh that's it!'

"As he said this he shot his load into her in several shuddering spasms. Then both drew their weapons from their respective sheaths and the girl wiped herself and put down her petticoats. This done she gave me a demure curtsey, and hoped that Mademoiselle had been amused. I gave her another crown and bid her adieu. Then, turning to Victor, I requested him to give Robert a bottle of wine, and tell him to ride behind in Victor's place, and share it with Phillippe. As to Victor, himself, I ordered him to come inside, as I had some messages to give him for my mother. As may be expected, all orders were cheerfully obeyed.

CHAPTER XI

"It is to be presumed that Robert and Phillippe enjoyed their wine in the rumble seat outside. If they did, my arrangement was most satisfactory to all parties. As for Victor, he seemed perfectly wild for joy at finding himself inside the carriage with me and Fanchette. I was not much less pleased, for my sensual feelings had been considerably excited by the little double game we had just witnessed, and my pretty Fanchette moved uneasily in her seat as if something had tickled her. I dare say she felt as if a strong flesh-pole driven into her would bolt her into her place comfortably enough.

"'I wonder how that poor girl feels by this time, Victor?' I said.

"'Rather moist but happy enough I dare say,' he replied, 'She has more money in her pocket than she ever had at one time before, and she has been right well drilled. A muscular but rather coarse, though undoubtedly handsome girl suits such unrefined fellows as Robert and Phillippe exactly. All they want is a rough, hairy cunt, a huge fat rump, with a hole big enough to be made use of in case of necessity or fancy, and a good wriggler with lots of spunk.'

"'And pray, sir, what more do you require, and what is the difference between you and them?' said I playfully.

"'I'll tell you, Mademoiselle," he replied. 'I admire a graceful, high-born girl, with a beautiful face and ruby lips with a bosom like snow and long graceful legs, and milk white thighs.' As he spoke he undressed me. By this time I was naked up to my belly. Immediately my elegant young page became busily engaged with his face between my thighs sucking and kissing my cunt. I don't know what Fanchette thought of all this, but she had sense enough to perceive that it was not the first time the handsome page and I had had familiar intercourse together. At least she knew that the mistress would be served before the maid. So she kept a discreet silence, with a good-humored smile on her face.

"I was pleased with her cheerfulness, and said: 'Never mind, Fanchette, you will have him to yourself all the way home again. Let me enjoy him while I can.'

"'Can I be of any assistance, my dear mistress?' she asked.

"'I don't know, Fanchette,' I replied. 'It all depends upon the style in which this young gentleman, who seems to have mistaken my cunt for a box of bon-bons, proposes to honor his young mistress by fucking her.'

"'For shame, Victor," said Fanchette. 'get off your knees, sir. Don't you see that Mademoiselle Emilie is beginning to want something better than that stupid head of yours between her thighs?'

"'Well,' said the page, withdrawing his face, 'if my beautiful mistress does not care about my head, she may about my tail. It is heartily at her service. Perhaps, dear Mademoiselle, if Fanchette were to hold

157

your dress completely up, and you would condescend to seat yourself in my lap, you would find it an agreeable way of being fucked, especially in a carriage.'

"This was a novelty to me, although I had thought that between Victor and Monsieur de Merville I'd had a pretty considerable experience of the different modes. So I gladly consented. Indeed, I would then have consented to almost anything resembling a good hearty fucking. I felt so thoroughly ripe for it. With Fanchette's assistance, I raised my clothes, and while she raised them up, I partly supported myself on her shoulders, straddling over the page's thighs until I settled my open buttocks on his lap.

"At this juncture Fanchette's assistance was invaluable. Seated in front of me she could witness the whole proceeding, and still keeping hold of my clothes with her left hand, with her right hand she guided the page's jerking cock into my burning parts. And oh! What a delightful relief it was to the gnawing lust I felt to have his great, stiff prick searching the inside of my cunt! I settled myself down upon him heavily. Though our motions were irregular, partly through my inexperience of the situation, and partly through the jolting motion of the carriage—though old Jacques, the coachman, who had a shrewd notion of what was going on inside, drove very slowly—the sensation to me was most delightful. Indeed I proved it by releasing my flood of passion all over Victor's cock and balls. As I sank forward on dear Fanchette's neck, I felt my partner give a last few vigorous forward shoves that spermed me well, and then he also sank back against the cushions in a speechless state of exhausted transport. When we separated, my kind assistant first of all wiped my dripping orifice, and then began to do the same to the carriage cushions, which she feared would tell a tale.

"'Never mind the cushions, Fanchette!' exclaimed Victor. "If Madame notices the stain, she will only

158

think it is in consequence of all the fucking you're going to receive on your journey homewards. Please wipe me dry instead.'

"'Indeed, Master Impudence, I shall do no such thing,' was her reply. Notwithstanding this, I noticed that she did so, and very delicately and carefully, too, handling his tool as if it was something very precious.

"This being finished, she turned to me and blushing prettily, said, 'Dear Mademoiselle Emilie, if you would condescend to look out the window for a few minutes, and if that proud and happy-looking sinner will shut his eyes, I should like to do something to myself. For indeed the delightful things I have just witnessed have put me into such a state of mind and body that I must have some relief. If I'd had any forethought I would have brought a tallow candle with me, but my fingers will be better than nothing. It is what many a poor neglected girl has to resort to. I cannot presume to ask such a favor as that young fellow fucking me in the presence of his Mistress, and besides I should think it would be half an hour, at the very least, before he was ready.'

"I laughingly said that I could promise for myself, but could not answer for my page. He also promised to be blind to her proceedings. without having, as I could plainly see, any intention of keeping his word. Then Fanchette—for I did not even pretend to look out of the window—leaned back in the corner of the carriage with her left foot placed upon the seat, and her right upon the floor. This position, when she had gathered up her clothes, made a nice open exposure and afforded a full view of her proceedings...or rather I should say her attempted proceedings, for she could not manage to accomplish her purposes at all. First she crammed her finger in her cunt, but the little useless thing produced irritation without satisfaction. Next, she tried her middle finger without much better result. Then she tried both together, and crammed them both in with all her might, wriggling and shifting her bottom about on the cushions in an uneasy and dissatisfied manner. At last she fairly burst out into tears of vexation and disappointment.

"The kind-hearted Victor could not bear to see a pretty girl in tears when he thought it possible to alleviate her distress. In a whisper he asked me if I would permit such a liberty in my presence and not consider it a cause for jealousy. He thought he could give Fanchette some satisfaction better than the useless child's play performance she was attempting, though he added he was too thoroughly exhausted himself to have any great pleasure.

"I replied out loud that I was no dog in the manger, that I myself had plenty to last me for another hour at least. I should be very glad indeed if he could give my little favorite some pleasure. She deserved it, I thought, for the cheerful way in which she had assisted us in our amorous performance, and for her general good temper.

"'Then mademoiselle,' said Victor, 'if Fanchette will kneel down before me and handle my tool, or even perhaps, if requisite, suck it a little, I think that under such delicate treatment he will be induced to hold up his head like a man and stiffen sufficiently to reward her liberally for the service she does me.'

"'What do you say, Fanchette?' said I to her.

"'Anything, my dear Mistress, that will relieve the craving I feel in my secret parts. I fear nothing but a cock will be of any service.'

"So saying, the excited girl flung herself on her knees before Victor and began pulling his breeches down with very little ceremony. That done, she pulled forth his prick and its balls, but with rather more care. It is worthy of remark that though Victor could not manage to stiffen his rod when first her hand touched him, his prick presented a swollen appearance...much larger than it would have been in a state of absolute quiescence, or about two-thirds the size it would be fully erect. I have reason to believe that this is a sign that sensual desire exists, and that the animal vitality is in full force, though latent.

"If I am wrong," continued Emilie, "I appeal to such experienced gentlemen as Father Eustace and Monsieur Auguste to correct me, especially the former."

"I beg to say," said the holy father, "that Emilie has made a very proper remark. An experienced surgeon could not have expressed himself better, and I shall be happy to show her how correct she is at any time she likes."

"I thank your Reverence," replied Emilie, very demurely. Then she continued: "Grasping Victor's tool in her right hand, Fanchette began to move her hand up and down, frigging him gently. It is my belief that if she had continued this patiently for five minutes she would have attained the desired stiffness without further trouble. But, poor girl, she had not patience. I heard her whisper, 'Darling Victor, how shall I present myself to you? And how soon will you be ready?' He replied that he thought if she would only go down on all fours on the floor of the carriage, it would be a nice easy position for her. 'Besides, you must know Fanchette,' he added, 'that the sight of a girl's wriggling posteriors produces a peculiar sensuality very exciting to a half worn out youth. I think I shall be ready in three minutes.'

"'Three minutes,' exclaimed the girl. 'Why it is an age.'

"'Perhaps, if you suck me, it will hasten proceedings,' suggested Victor.

"The only answer Fanchette made to this was to instantly take his prick into her mouth, and, as it seemed to me, to half swallow it. I could see her cheeks swell as she laved his cock well with her tongue. The good effects of this fresh proceeding were

161

immediately apparent: Victor began to heave on his side, and I, who narrowly and perhaps rather jealously watched the activities, noticed that his eyes began to sparkle. Presently he said, "Now, my sweet girl, on your hands and knees as quickly as you like."

"Fanchette immediately adopted the required posture. Wanting to assist her as she had assisted me, I pulled her clothes towards me so as to bare the lower part of her body up to the waist. Then putting my hands to her buttocks I pulled open both her orifices so that Victor might have his choice; he chose cunt, decidedly what I consider the proper place, though of course, circumstances may alter cases. Or he might have thought he did not have the force and stiffness requisite for the smaller hole. Anyway, he effected a beautiful entrance, gentle and sliding, partly I dare say to be attributed to the workmanlike way in which I held the lips open for him. At first I thought he did not intend to do more than give my pretty attendant pleasure, and reserve his regenerated sperm flood for me perhaps. But his lust seemed to increase with every additional shove. I thought less of my own interests and encouraged his thrusts with such remarks as, 'Well done, Victor! What a nice springy rump she has, has she not? What nice round thighs! What a jolly little bum-hole! That's right. Shove in up to the balls!'

"I only perceived my imprudence when Fanchette completely finished and let down her flowing cream. I thought Victor would then withdraw and reserve himself for his young mistress. But no! He was getting into his work, and was commencing half lingering pushes. Fanchette now actually threw one of her arms around my left leg for support, to prevent herself being shoved head first through the carriage door, I suppose. Victor continued to pump, varying the speed and length of his strokes. He jiggled from side to side so as to stretch the clutching cunt lips, then resumed his plunges. At length the page concluded his lascivious exercises, giving one heavy thrust and remaining in the warm sheath, while he leaned so heavily upon his pretty companion that she could hardly support his weight. When he condescended to withdraw his weapon and rise before even buttoning himself, he suggested refreshing ourselves with a flask of champagne, which he took from a basket dragged from under the carriage seat. This we gratefully accepted, and I praised his forethought, and I asked him if he would not take some himself. He replied in the negative, saying he would take some brandy with old Jacques, the coachman. It would serve to put the old fellow in good humor, and also would have a better appearance, for we were approaching the village where we were to dine, and it would look unbecoming for him to be found riding inside with his young mistress, though even by her own express orders. This was so prudent and thoughtful that I had nothing to say against it, and approved of his doing as he proposed.

"Very shortly afterwards we reached the village inn, where I was received by the host with all the deference due to a young lady of high family. Moreover I was greatly pleased to find that my Mother had sent forward a courier on horseback to order dinner to be ready for our party on arrival.

"This was more than I expected from her, and the result was that we were served with speed and comfort. I, of course, had my family atten-dant...Victor...dine with me. When I had nearly finished my repast I heard a considerable disturbance, which seemed to come from the inn kitchen. I was thinking of requesting Victor to ascertain the meaning of it when in rushed the landlady in a high state of terror and indignation.

"'Ah, Mademoiselle,' she exclaimed, 'those footmen of yours are devils! Real devils incarnate! They are taking indecent liberties with my chambermaid and my kitchenmaid, who are two good girls quite innocent with regard to such romps. One of them kissed my

163

daughter Rosalie and swore she was a very pretty girl, and had the impudence to ask her if her lips between her thighs were as sweet as those of her face!'

"'Why does not your husband interfere, my good woman?' said I, 'and what can a weak girl as I am do among two or three lustful men?'

"'My husband!' exclaimed the hostess in shrill and indignant tones. 'Confound him! He was drinking hard cider with the courier all morning 'til he was more than half fuddled; now, some wine those wretches have given him has made him helplessly drunk, and he thinks these horrible proceedings are all fun and games. He sits and laughs like an imbecile.'

"Mademoiselle's old coachman sits by the fireside smoking his pipe, to all appearances indifferent if half the province fucked the other half. But if Mademoiselle would descend into the kitchen and interfere by interposing her authority and order the abominable ravishers out of the house and into the stable, then decency might be preserved.'

"To keep up appearances I prepared to descend, knowing perfectly well from what I had heard about Parisian footmen, and what I had myself seen of the behavior of Robert and Phillippe as we passed thru the forest that I stood a very small chance of being listened to, especially if their lusts were seriously excited. A little rough play no girl would mind, and of course I could not object to it. Moreover I hoped that as the noise had almost if not altogether ceased, we should not find matters in the kitchen quite so bad as the landlady had reported.

So I asked Fanchette to retire into my bedroom and told Victor to follow me. I marched downstairs looking as authoritarian and majestic as I could. But, alas! when I arrived at the kitchen door I found all my majestic airs thrown away. I had to save my threats and remonstrances for some other occasion.

The noise of struggling and squealing and romping had ceased, sure enough, for the minute the old lady turned her back those clever rascals, Robert and Phillippe had taken matters a step further. Antoine, the courier, who had been making hot love to Rosalie, the landlady's daughter, ever since his arrival, had persuaded her that now or never was the time to make him happy with her love. The consequence of this was that when I swept majestically into the kitchen and was just beginning to say, 'Robert and Phillippe! what do you mean?' when all of a sudden I stopped as if paralyzed by what I saw.

"A plump rosy faced girl was on her hands and knees on the dresser, and Robert was fucking her as if his salvation depended upon his banging her rump black and blue. Phillippe had got a tall, Gypsy looking girl (the chamber-maid I suppose) leaning with her face against the pantry door, with her buttocks stuck out! He was fucking her mare fashion. But whether he was confining himself to legitimate fucking I could not tell, and most certainly did not ask. My opinion is he was getting in anywhere he could find a hole. But worst of all, and a sight most shocking to the motherly eyes of my landlady, was the sight of her Rosalie, really a very handsome girl—with pretensions to ladylike manners—with her long well dressed legs contentedly crossed over the back of Antoine, our courier. He was fucking Rosalie as contentedly and heartily as if they had just been married and had retired to their bridal couch with the blessings of their parents and relatives! But instead he was violating a young girl whom he had never seen before, on a table in the middle of the kitchen, in broad daylight, under the nose of her father and mother and a dozen other people besides! Here was a pretty state of things!

"The old lady gave one shriek of rage and horror, and seizing a broomstick was doubtless going to annihilate everything and everybody, beginning with her husband, who was staggering forward to depreciate her wrath by explaining, I presume, that the young folks were only amusing each other.

"That would have had his skull cracked I doubt not. only just as the blow was about to descend, old Jacques gave him an adroit shove and toppled him over on his hands and knees right in front of his wife. She screamed out for help, and as Jacques stepped forward I thought he was going to help her up. This I considered as a pity, as she would only cause more violence and confusion, and could not possibly mend matters, much less maidenheads. But I did my worthy old coachman an injustice; instead of helping her up, he deliberately seated himself upon her. While his solid weight kept the half-stunned old woman from rising, he calmly smoked his pipe, and looked benignly around him as if he were a benefactor to his species. Upon my word the mere recollection of this absurd climax to this indecent scene makes me laugh.

"When Victor perceived the masterstroke of policy performed by old Jacques, he called out to the other young fellows, 'Make haste now, you abominable ravishers, and put your fair friends out of their pain. You are a lucky fellow, Antoine, to make good with such a pretty lady-like girl to fuck. But if you do not look sharp and get on your saddle, you will find yourself very unlucky, for old Jacques cannot sit on the old woman all day. When she gets up she will most assuredly avenge her daughter's lost maidenhead, by giving you a broken head with that broom, or a poker, or some other cheerful instrument. The other girls don't so much matter.'

"On hearing this Antoine, who had finished Rosalie, and was only luxuriously resting on her snow-white belly, while his prick lay soaking in its pretty sheath, at once arose, and hurried out to the stables, buttoning himself up as he went. As Rosalie lay back exhausted with her clothes still up, and her cunt wide open, I took compassion on her helplessness and assisted her off the table, telling her to go up to my room, and instructing her to tell my maid to wash her and assist her in arranging her dress. I promised to join her directly. I hinted to Victor and Jacques that they should join me in asserting to the old lady that her daughter had been sitting with my waiting maid in my chamber during the last half hour, and that Antoine set out for Paris as soon as he finished his dinner. The idea of bullying the old lady out of the evidence of her own eyes tickled them amazingly, and they readily adopted the idea, promising to communicate with Robert and Phillippe.

"These rogues, it appeared, had not been satisfied with one fuck each. When they had concluded the first round, they agreed to change partners. Phillippe had taken the girl which Robert had just finished, and laying her down flat on her face on the dresser, rammed into her fat rump in his usual beastly style; while Robert keeping Phillippe's chamber-maid, pinned up against the door did not behave much better as he reamed her arse.

"But all fucking, even of the most varied character, must come to an end, and both these rogues seemed fairly exhausted when they drew their pricks out of their respective sheaths. As they buttoned up and applied themselves to the brandy bottle, I told them to give the poor girls some, and left them with Victor and Jacques to stupefy the half-stunned landlady. I proceeded upstairs to my chamber and found Rosalie looking very much refreshed. A glass of champagne completed her restoration, and when I told her of the story I had ordered my men to palm off upon her mother, she was exceedingly grateful, and exclaimed that I was an angel of mercy.

"It was now near time for our departure, and I summoned Victor to have the horses put to the carriage, and make everything ready for our departure. He came up and said that he had already taken it upon himself to do so, as he feared that if Robert and Phillippe drank any more brandy they would become drunk and useless. He also reported that, as to the family servants, the worthy hostess did not seem to care if they had been fucked until their two holes were knocked into one. But she was very indignant about her daughter, and did not half believe her story about her absence upstairs, evidently being under the impression that she had run off with that villain of a debauched Parisian courier.

"On this a pretty idea struck me. 'Fanchette,' said I, 'take Rosalie downstairs with you and assure the hostess of the truth of the statement that she has been here half an hour or so, and that Antoine has been gone any time you like to mention. Take my purse with you, and settle the account liberally; that will put her in a good humor. And give those two severely fucked girls a small present.'

"Do you see, my friends, how cleverly I managed to clear the room of the two girls and keep my maid some short time downstairs too? Of course, Master Victor did not hurry himself to leave the room. On the contrary, when he had seen the two girls fairly out, he shut and bolted the door. I, knowing that there was no time for any nonsense, had already taken up my clothes and laid myself on my back on the outside of the bed with my knees up and my thighs wide open!

"'Oh! when shall I ever see such charms again!' exclaimed the enraptured page, as he pressed his lips alternately to my lips, my bosom, my limbs, and my cunt, 'So white, so delicate, and yet so agile, and so passionately warm!" So saying he leaped on the bed, and got between my thighs, and viewed with delight the mossy orifice he designed to enter. Then gently placing the shining knob between the lips, he threw

168

forward the whole weight of his body, and I felt his balls right up against my bottom at the very first shove. Whether the dear fellow thought that it was the last fuck or not that he was going to get out of me, I don't know; but he seemed determined it would be a good one. Twice I thought he was going to finish me. But he restrained himself, resting as it were, and only gave slight and gentle pushes. Then he collected himself for a final effort, he seemed to inject his very life and soul into me in the shape of warm jetting cream.

"Before we parted he vowed and declared that he loved me better than his life, and that, whether he remained at my mother's house or not, he would find the means to hear if I left the convent. Then we prudently resolved to have no more communication with each other until I arrived at the holy place. This resolution we strictly adhered to with the exception of a warm pressure of the hand which I received as he assisted me to leave the carriage at the gates.

"The remainder of my story since entering your house," she concluded to the Mother Superior, "you, my honored lady, know as well as I can tell you. Suffice it to say in concluding my long and tedious story, that I have been much happier here than ever I expected to be—and have had infinitely more pleasure than I could ever have dreamed of."

CHAPTER XII

When Emilie had concluded her narrative there was a little hesitation among us, her circle of listeners, as to whether we should have another story from some other of the party, or whether we should adjourn. My aunt, the Lady Abbess, was decidedly in favor of the latter. She seemed to think that although the ladies present, nuns, novices and visitors—might be inclined to listen to such stories all the afternoon (for, of course, it was now pretty far advanced), the health and good looks of the girls under her charge would be better promoted by their retiring or amusing themselves by walking in the garden until supper time. For this purpose she requested Adele to convey her commands to her housekeeper, or a lay sister who acted in that capacity, to provide a good supper for the young ladies present in the sitting room appropriated for the novices and young lady boarders. Then she and my mother withdrew to her chamber.

Father Eustace invited me to follow him to a comfortable room, which he called a "cell" that was appropriated for his use whenever his duty or his pleasure, or both, required him to take up his residence at the convent. This apartment seemed at first view very commonly furnished, but a further inspection showed it was only so outwardly. The bed, which was covered with a grass rug, was large, and warm and soft; the elbow chair, which was clumsy and ugly to look at was a very easy one to sit in; and though there was no carpet on the floor, a thick soft mat served the purpose as well or even better. On the walls of the room, ostentatiously displayed among pictures of saints and angels, were a coarse hair shirt and a knotted whip. In a private drawer, which his reverence unlocked for me, was a supple rod of birch twigs, and some straps and buckles lying among a lot of colored pictures of the most licentious and lust-exciting character. I could easily guess that the holy father made much more frequent and agreeable use of his concealed property than that which was openly displayed. There was a portable bath in the room, which he recommended me to use, saying that there was nothing like it for promoting the restoration of one's cock.

"Dash plenty of cold water over your rump and private parts, my son," said he, "The more your cock shrinks up from the chilling treatment, the more ready will it be to stand erect when called upon. And you really have done very good work today...as much, I think, as I could have done in my very best days, and I was very celebrated among my penitents, rather a favorite confessor, I flatter myself. Let me see! You fucked Emilie first thing this morning, then you and she worked on Louise's feelings until she was silly enough to let you take her maidenhead. Then there was that abominable imposition upon sister Agnes that was partly my Lady Agatha's doings. If I had thought that was anything of that kind going on in that quarter, I would have spoken to you about it

171

beforehand, Master Auguste, for I had intended to have the gratification of taking that young lady's virginity myself; there's a racy and piquant feeling in breaking into the sanctuary of a piously disposed prudish girl like Agnes. Tell me did she make a good fuck? Did she wriggle her rump well about?"

I explained to him that we were obliged to strap her to the bedpost at first, but that when my ready attendants perceived that she appreciated the amusement they set her legs free, and then she became very active and quite excited.

"Ah! so I should have thought. She has very fine buttocks," added he in a musing tone. "You buggered her very nicely this afternoon; I was not so busily engaged serving your magnificent mother with the same sauce that I didn't have time to notice it. It was a very creditable performance indeed," continued he, nodding his head with approbation, "particularly in a couple of novices. Well, let me see, that makes three, or rather I should say four, if you count the rump performance. By the way, you fucked Adele mare fashion, didn't you? And she was giving her Mother Superior satisfaction with a dildo. Well that makes five. Good enough, young gentleman, for one day. But I would not recommend you, my son, to look too much at those charming pictures. They are beginning to make your cock stand again, already! Really, you are a very fine boy, and exactly what I was like at your age."

These remarks were produced by my examining the collection of lascivious pictures, while I was industriously rubbing myself with a coarse towel. The two stimulants together were certainly producing the effect that my spiritual (and real) father had noticed. I told him to never mind appearances, that I should be all right after supper, but at the same time asked him if he could not from his secret stores produce some tonic to stimulate the appetite, as I did not feel very strong in that particular. He smilingly replied that he had everything in his cell that could contribute to man's comfort, except a woman, and that he could have for the asking. So saying, he produced a small bottle, and mixing a spoonful of its contents with an equal quantity of wine, bade me drink it. The draught was slightly bitter but not unpalatable. The effect was undeniable, and perceptible in the short space of ten minutes.

"You are right, my son," remarked the monk in reply to my expressions of approval, "it is a most valuable restorative, and I have found it most useful as a stimulant. The secret was confided to me by an apothecary to his late Majesty who found it of great benefit in restoring his worn out energies, and in exciting sensual desires in the minds of virtuous young ladies for whom he designed the honor of a real fucking. As a page of honor to his Majesty I saw a good deal of that kind of thing, and if I had confined myself to merely seeing, I should not now be a monk. But alas! Temptation overcame prudence, and one day I committed myself seriously. I need not tell you, my son, that even the ordinary footmen of ladies of quality see a good deal of the private life of the families with whom they are domesticated; what then must be the opportunities of a favored page of a king's be among the ladies of his Majesty's court?

"Now among the king's favorites there were a great many still untouched, waiting for the happy time to arrive when they would be honored by making the acquaintance of the royal cock. Among these was a certain young lady of high family. Julie St. Roche, whom I could not help fancying often cast a longing eye upon the handsome page, namely myself—and I was speedily convinced of it. It happened thus. The king was giving a court ball at which all the handsome ladies were expected to be present, and he selected among his favorites those of high

173

family who would not shock the aristocratic feeling of the nobility who would be present. You will understand that morality, or modesty, or virtue, were trifles of no consequence at all. He selected me to be the bearer of his commands to such of his pets as lived out of Paris at his country home. Among others I carried a message to Mademoiselle St. Roche.

"Glad of a change of scene, and, moreover, of a ball with all its attendant fine dresses, music and voluptuous dances, Julie was in ecstasy; she showed it by kissing me over and over again as the bearer of such good news. There was only one other young lady present—Mademoiselle La Fontaine. She was equally delighted but more prudent, saying:

"'Mind what you are doing, Julie, kissing that young fellow! Recollect that he is something more than a boy, as perhaps he will show you if you excite his manly propensities!'

"At this Julie only blushed and laughed, and said that her friend was a prude. She insisted that I was a boy and only a boy, and so young that I could not possibly do any mischief.

"'Maybe so,' said the other young lady who retired, remarking that we go to her wardrobe to look for a suitable ball dress. The moment her back was turned, I considered that I ought in common gratitude to return Julie some of the kisses she had given me, which I did with such head and force as to inspire her with a greater respect for my manly powers than she professed to have had previously. Then I told her that I believed his Majesty desired some sensual honor on the coming occasion. On hearing this she colored up, and asked me in the same breath what I meant, and how I knew. I informed her that I had been waiting at table at a private supper which my master had given to old Madame Desart, whom Julie well knew, as she had been the means of introducing her to the king. His Majesty was consulting this elderly procuress as to the different charms and capabilities of the untried ladies of his seraglio, and she had strongly recommended Mademoiselle St. Roche.

"'Indeed, sweet lady,' said I, 'she spoke so rapturously of your various charms, of your beautiful white bosom, of your long well-shaped legs, of your round white rump and of the virgin treasure you cherish between your milk white thighs, that she quite raised my curiosity as well as the king's.'

"'Indeed, Master Eustace,' said she, 'and what do you think he will do to me?'

"'I know,' said I.

"'You do?' she exclaimed in surprise, 'How?'

"'I was on duty in the ante-chamber the first time he had an interview with Mademoiselle La Fontaine, the young lady who has just left the room, and I peeped through the curtain that overhung the door, and I saw—'

"'What?' eagerly asked my fair companion. 'Dear Eustace, do tell me!'

"'In this wicked world, fair lady,' I replied 'one never gives anything for nothing. But I will tell you all about the pretty spectacle I witnessed, if you will permit me to have one peep at those magnificent charms which Madam Desart so enthusiastically described.'

"'Pages are always saucy,' replied the laughing girl, 'but you are such a child that I suppose there will be no great harm in your having one peep; but recollect, sir, if you please, that it is only to be peeping, not handling.'

"'Oh, of course not, beautiful Julie,' said I. With that, as she was standing up, I went down on one knee and raised the wide spreading flounces of her dress. I began to lift up the undergarments. One of the great charms of my investigation was that since these treasured ladies were liable at any time to

175

receive his Majesty's embraces, so they were always dressed to perfection as to their petticoats and chemises. In the present case I first of all viewed a vista of long white silk stocking, leading to a splendid regalia of creamy thighs and rump. I pulled the thighs and cheeks of her posteriors apart, rather roughly I fear (so much for not handling), and began kissing, licking, and sucking her brown-haired cunt with all the passionate ardor of a seventeen-year-old. She liked it, I'm sure, for she not only made no resistance, but opened her thighs and stooped a little so that I had a fair chance to insert my finger into her charming orifice.

"Of a sudden she exclaimed, 'Stop, dear Eustace, I hear somebody coming!' Instantly, but most unwillingly, I emerged from my delightful hiding place, and placed myself in a respectful attitude, while she sat down, looking as innocent as she could. The somebody, whoever it was, walked pass the door however, without even looking in, and then we breathed more freely.

"'And now, Eustace,' said the lovely girl, 'since you have had your inspection, and a taste too, I should think, you are bound to tell me what you saw his gracious Majesty doing to my friend La Fontaine.'

"'Certainly, Mademoiselle,' I replied. 'Only promise me not to be vexed with me if, in my description and illustrations, I shock your notions of delicacy.'

"'Oh, certainly not!' replied she.

"'Very well, then,' replied I. 'The first thing his Majesty did was demand my assistance in taking down his royal breeches, and bringing to view his sacred tool, thus,' said I, suiting the action to the word and allowing my own garments to disclose to the astonished Julie a very respectfully sized prick for a boy of seventeen, and stiff enough to poke a hole through a dead board.

"'Bless me what a pretty thing!' said the innocent

176

girl, taking hold of it, 'and has the king got an instrument like this? And what does he do with it?'

"'That Mademoiselle, I am about to explain to you,' replied I, with as much gravity as I could command. 'When he had thus prepared himself, he ordered me to retire and usher in Mademoiselle La Fontaine.'

"When I introduced the young lady I did not retire far, but drawing the curtains of the anteroom (where no one but I was allowed to enter) about one inch apart and watched the whole proceeding. You will be interested to know, Mademoiselle, that your fair friend lay herself on the sofa in very nearly the same attitude in which you are now placed, only her legs were drawn up a little, and her thighs more spread—something in this manner,' said I, putting her limbs in the posture I described. I wondered that her common-sense did not suggest the impropriety of my taking such liberties with her; but the fact of the case is, her animal passions had gained supremacy over her, and, for the time, she had no common sense.

"'Then, sweet Julie,' I continued, 'the king lifted her silk robe and her snowy underclothing up to her waist, thus revealing charms as snowy as the garments that veiled them. Very lovely I thought the sight then, but it was not nearly so beautiful as the prospect which now fires every drop of blood in my veins.'

"The only reply that Julie could make to this statement was a long drawn sigh. Perceiving I was not likely to meet with much resistance, if any, I hastily concluded with, 'and then his Majesty did this.' As I made this last remark, I pulled open the ruby lips of Julie's delicious cunt, still moist from my licking and sucking, and placing myself on the sofa between her thighs, guiding the scarlet oval top of my gallant young prick into the orifice of her lips. I

177

flung my weight forward upon her and let my cock find its way in.

"At this forcible illustration of the scene I had witnessed between my royal master and Mademoiselle La Fontaine, Julie gave a slight scream, but she had just sense enough left to know that any exclamation of alarm might bring unwelcome intruders upon the scene. Moreover, I smothered her face with kisses to such an extent that screaming was not very easy.

"Previous to this I had speared two or three chambermaids—somehow or other it seems to be considered part of the duty of a court page to do so—but I had never before fucked a young lady of rank, or taken a maidenhead. Now I was doing both at once, and, oh, how delicious it was! How I revelled in her delicate charms. How I grieved when my ecstasy came to an end and I shot a stream of pearly nectar into her violated pussy. I longed to remain in her, feeling sure that within ten minutes I would be able to go to work again with fresh vigor. But it was midday, the room was liable to be entered at any moment. For the sake of my fair partner I rose and put my disordered garments straight.

"But Mademoiselle St. Roche forgot to be equally careful; she lay back exhausted, just as I had left her, with her petticoats up, her thighs open, and the creamy foam over the brown hair and ruby lips of her gaping cunt. And, of course Mademoiselle La Fontaine chose that very moment to enter!

"'Well, Julie,' said she, 'here is a pretty picture. What are you doing in that horribly indelicate position, with your clothes up? And you, master page, what are you doing here?'

"I bowed respectfully, and replied that Mademoiselle St. Roche had been troubled with an abominable flea, and that we had been trying to catch it.

"'I fear, Master Page, that you have been searching for fleas in very improper places.' she gravely replied. 'But what induced you to think it possible for a flea to be up that little orifice, which looks as if it is no longer so little?'

"From the tone of her conversation I saw that it was of no use to attempt to deceive her, and was at a loss what to say. Julie beckoned me to her, and while her friend wondered what she could be saying, whispered to me that she would engage her in conversation and beg her not to disclose what she had just seen. At the same time she would carelessly clasp her arms around her neck, and hold her fast in a stooping position. While she was thus situated, it would be easy and pleasant for me to get into her from behind, "And then you'll be sure, Eustace dear, that she will not be able to tell stories of us!"

I had always heard that women were apt learners in these matters, but I must acknowledge that I was perfectly astonished at the extraordinary diplomatic talent exhibited by the hitherto inexperienced Julie. I considered her idea a very good one, and without waiting for my assent she proceeded to put it into practice.

"'Dear Adelaide, come here, I want to speak to you,' said she.

"'Well, what is it, you silly, imprudent girl?' replied her friend approaching her and leaning over her.

"This was all Julie needed. She clasped her white arms around Adelaide's neck, and drew her face down to hers began to beg her in an audible whisper not to breathe a word of the suspicious appearance of matters when she so suddenly entered the room.

"'Of course I shall not, my pet,' replied La Fontaine. 'It would only bring scandal upon our little community, and make the king and our abominable old governess look more sharply after us. But, gra-

179

cious heavens!' she continued, 'what is that impudent page doing?'

"You will observe, my son, that as she promised not to reveal her suspicions there was no necessity for me to purchase her secrecy by violating her. But secrecy or not, my fancy had been stimulated, and as Mademoiselle La Fontaine leaned over her friend, the position raised the skirt of her silken flounces so as to exhibit her legs in a most captivating manner. Her exclamation was caused by my putting my head under her petticoats to obtain a nearer and more extensive view. When she called out, the only alteration I made in my proceedings was to stand up, raising her petticoats with my head as I did so. My faithful Julie kept tight hold of her at the same time, so she was perfectly harmless as far as any resistance was concerned, and her position stuck her buttocks out in such a way as to render either of the two crevices nestling in the neighborhood easy prey to my roving prick. I have fucked many a pretty girl since, my dear boy, and many a lady of rank has considered herself honored by having accepted my loving embraces, but I shall never forget the day I took a young lady's maidenhead for the first time, or the first time that the idea struck me that a girl's bottom-hole must be a delightful change.

"At any rate, whether impelled by novelty, or curiosity, or by lust, or Adelaide's tempting position, or all four, I certainly was not disappointed. At first I thought her tightness would baffle me but I supplied the remedy by moistening the end of my prick with saliva. When I tried again, I forced the knob in with one vigorous shove. That done, the rest of the performance was easy; the remainder of my cock followed, and in two lunging thrusts was buried up to my balls.

"Adelaide did not pretend to resist but simply remarked to her friend, 'You have played a nice trick, you naughty girl! See if I don't pay you back for it? In the meantime you will excuse me for remarking that this saucy page of yours is a lascivious and unnaturally lustful young beast.'

"'Unnatural!' exclaimed Mademoiselle St. Roche. 'Why you don't mean he has inserted—"

"'Yes, I do mean to say,' interrupted Adelaide, 'and it is just as well that he is quite a youth and has not grown to full size, for if he had a full grown thick prick, such as I have seen and felt, I would run some risk of having my bottomhole split. And now, after three or four more thrusts I suppose his Highness is finished; yes, I thought so. Many thanks to you, Monsieur, for the distinguished honor you have done my posteriors!" said the laughing girl, turning around as I withdrew myself. 'Julie, if you'll take my advice you'll come upstairs with me, while this lovely young gentleman gets into the saddle and back again to Paris. For if this escapade should happen to be noticed, you and I will be disgraced forever; while the page here will run a very good chance of being castrated. I suppose he thinks that would be a pity, while my own opinion is that it would save the maidenheads of a number of poor innocent girls.'

"I saw her advice, though given in a laughing tone, was correct and quite serious. Consequently, kissing both young ladies warmly, I spurred my horse at full gallop on the return to Paris. And it was well I did so, for the king was terribly jealous, as worn-out tyrants usually are, and had already noticed I had been longer on the road than he expected. I averted suspicion from myself by entering into long descriptions of the enthusiasm with which the young ladies had received the invitation of the royal fete, and the flattering and grateful remarks they had made about his Majesty. I even improvised a sort of half-angry, half-jealous conversation, which I pretended to have overheard among some of the beauties, contending as to which of them was the most likely to be honored by his royal embraces. This, which was all fiction from beginning to end, pleased the king vastly; and I flattered myself that I had re-established myself in his good graces.

"But I overlooked something. It seems that the Governess of the country villa had a nephew, a bastard son, whom she wished to place as a Royal page. As there was no vacancy, she had to make one. The old harridan had not seen any of my delicious proceedings with my lovely friends, but she knew that they had been with me a considerable time. Taking that fact in connection with the use that both Julie and Adelaide made of a sponge on their reaching their apartments, she made a shrewd guess at the truth. She was pretty well versed in these little matters.

"The consequence of her suspicion was that she sought an audience with the king in Paris; and warned him against me as a dangerous youth to be let loose among his favorite women. She did not dare to accuse me of any impropriety, as she knew that their influence would outweigh hers; but a page who was present subsequently told me that she asserted that, whenever I approach any of his Majesty's treasured pets, I was afflicted with a terrible erection. The experienced old lady warned the king that a youth in that predicament does not stop to weigh the consequences, and she feared that some day my lust would lead me to attempt a rape on one of her charges, or at any rate would probably lead me to take extremely improper liberties.

"The king, perfectly horror-stricken at the idea of any ordinary person touching, or even thinking of invading the sanctuaries sacred to his royal prick, summoned me forthwith into his presence, and told me of what I was accused.

"On any other occasion I should have indignantly protested against any such accusation, and defied the scheming old hag to her face. But as it was, knowing myself to be guilty, I was afraid that any investigation might lead to worse results—the ruin of the ladies, and very possibly death to myself. So I answered respectfully that in common with all gallant young gentlemen in his gracious Majesty's service, I like to look at beautiful young ladies. But I had too much respect for those reserved for his Majesty's pleasure to presume to let my animal passions get the better of me in regard to them.

"To this the king shook his head doubtfully, and replied that I might be telling the truth, but that he feared he could not trust me. The temptation was too strong. If I desired to have the honor of continuing in his service, he suggested I submit to castration. To this I humbly objected; replying that I was as my maker had been pleased to make me, and much as I coveted and appreciated the honor of continuing in his royal service, I considered that at my age castration might cause death. Well, on this the king was very angry, and said that he had no doubt the suspicions about me were founded on fact. Since I seemed to be unworthy of the honor of continuing in his service, I should be made a monk, and enjoy myself in the seclusion of a monastery of the strictest order. But in some things the cowl is even stronger than the crown, and I had some friends in the church, who interfered. I was placed in a monastery of exceedingly easy discipline, where there were a considerable number of young monks of good family. From them I learned that monastic life has its charms and privileges as well as those of any other life, and in fact, that was the way I became a monk."

I had been rather curious to know how it was that a fine, handsome, strong man had adopted a line of life for which he was apparently so ill-suited. Apparently his proper sphere would have been at the head of a troop of heavy dragoons or a company of musketeers. I suggested to him that some of his penitents must have made exceedingly interesting confes-

183

sions to him, and that some pleasant adventures must have occurred in consequence.

"You are right, my son," he replied, "and according to our strict rule I ought not to divulge any such stories. But the fact is, our rules are growing weaker and weaker day by day, and I shall not be at all surprised to find very soon that there are no more rules or convents, or nuns, or priests in existence. So, by way of concluding your education, I shall have no hesitancy in divulging whatever in my experience I have found entertaining. Only I think in common fairness to our beautiful and accommodating companions they should hear this as well. Good Lord!" he continued in a musing tone, "what a series of adventures that girl Emilie did relate to us! For a girl of her age she has seen and experienced a great deal! And what a splendid young lady she is. I am glad to hear that she has been thoroughly well-fucked both back and front, for, as you may have noticed; my son, I am rather well hung, and I don't like hurting either my pretty companion, or myself.

"Adele, also, makes a very tidy fuck, I dare say, and I know she has acquired the art of satisfying the Superior, so she pleases somebody even if she is not big enough for me. Only, my son, if in the course of your innocent familiarity, you should happen to penetrate the precincts of her rump," here he winked knowingly, "just inform your spiritual director, will you?" He laughed.

"And apropos to this subject, my son," he continued, "whom do you propose to make your partner for the evening, or you bed-fellow for the night. What sort of a girl have you a fancy for? You shall have her if she is in the establishment, for my influence here is unlimited. The girls you have seen are all very pretty and sweet. But Agnes and Louise are undoubtedly sore, and will be better off sleeping alone. The Lady Abbess will want Adele. Emilie I mean to keep for myself; she has raised my lusts to a very high pitch by her spirited narrative; and I hope to fuck her in every shape and way, and in such positions as were never done either by Victor or the Vicomte de Merville!"

I replied that if my aunt wanted me again as she had the night before, I was bound in duty and in gratitude for her hospitality to give her the benefit of my humble performances.

But the monk here interrupted me with, "Duty hah! gratitude—bosh! Her handsome ladyship must not be too greedy. If she is, I will send for my friend, Father Ambrose, from the Franciscan Monastery closed by, and he shall serve her to her heart's content. It is not the first time that he has done so."

"No indeed," said I, "I have heard of her first adventure, struggling and straddling between Father Ambrose in front and your Reverence behind!"

"Ah," said he, smacking his lips, "that was nice! How young and active and tight she was." Then he sighed. "Yes, my son, enjoy yourself in the full bloom of your youth: Lord knows it comes to an end quickly enough and you can barely raise your cock with the urging of your own hand.

I smiled at this and thanked him, knowing that my stay at the Convent of Ste. Claire would be memorable indeed. Then we adjourned to the Lady Superior's apartment, where supper—and more—awaited us.

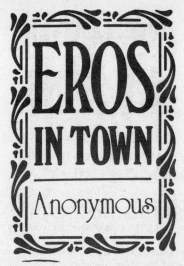

A selection of Erotica
from Headline